The Messenger

Donland and The Hornet

By

Perry Comer

DEDICATION

for

Jake Tabb

BOOKS BY PERRY COMER (Allan Brooks)

The Prize
(Naval Adventure)

The Messenger
(Donland and the Hornet)

Donland's Ransom
Donland and the Hornet

No Chance
(Young Adult - Coming of Age)

The Snake Killer
(Juvenile Action/adventure)

God's Broken Man
(Allan Brooks) (Christian Fiction)

Myrtle Beach Murder
(Allan Brooks)(Christian Fiction)

Fall of Fort Fisher
(Juvenile action/adventure)
(Civil War)

Andrew's War
(Juvenile action/adventure)
(Civil War)

Myrtle Beach Stories (Allan Brooks)
(Young Adult - Coming of Age)

What Jesus Said
(Sermon Outlines)

Chapters

CHAPTER ONE

March 1779

The coolness of the old stone walled café with a low-beamed ceiling was a pleasant place to wait out the squall. Two merchants sat at one table with a ledger between them, at another table, two young midshipmen ate cheese and bread with tots of rum. A very dour Spaniard with a shaggy head of black hair, rotten teeth and tattered clothes slumped against a wall waiting to fetch whatever the patrons should order. The cook, a dark-skinned woman, round and very plump, stood at the kitchen door.

Jackson chewed with delight. Roasted chicken and new potatoes with sautéed carrots were not the seaman's usual fare. Nor was the expensive Madeira. Hard weevil-laced biscuits and salt pork were the staples of the lower deck. If he were lucky, the water he was given aboard ship would not have vermin swimming in it.

Donland watched his friend and waited for him to swallow. "Admiral Welles said he would convene a board for your examination in a few days. Will you be ready?"

Jackson swallowed, lifted his glass and drained the contents. "Aye, ready for neigh on two years," he answered, then asked, "How many others?"

"I have the impression that only you are to be examined. It does occur from time to time that an admiral will convene a board as a formality to fulfill a favor or put forth one of his lackeys. In your case, my suspicion is that he wants rid of *Hornet.* Better she is at sea and the fever with her before it can spread to the other ships. And there is something else, something he will spring on us when the time suits him. The man is calculating."

"Aye, I've chanced a conversation or more with others. They swear the man is as cunning as a fox and as hard as iron."

"Like as not, like as not," Donland said absent-minded. His attention was drawn to a man about his own age wearing with a lace neckerchief and lace cuffs escorting a red-haired young lady wearing a lavender dress and matching bonnet. It wasn't Betty Sumerford, but the hair was the same.

Jackson didn't miss the resemblance and stated, "Sailed for Boston, so I was told."

Donland didn't respond.

"*Hornet* is out there biding her time," Jackson said a little louder.

Donland faced his friend, "Aye."

"More prize money won't come amiss," Jackson stated.

Donland grinned, "A lieutenant's pay is what you will be seeing and you'll think you are rich. Prize money is not in our future, old son; *Hornet* will do well to capture an island trader or two on this station. Our admiral will keep us busy chasing down smugglers and run-away slaves. He might on occasion send us as an escort, but that would be the oddity. Frigates are an independent command; free and swift, sloops are admiral's pawns to run errands."

"Aye, they are," Jackson said as he took a gulp of wine. He wiped his lips with the back of his hand.

Donland was staring at the back of the red-haired beauty.

"Free and independent so the lady is. She'll have forgotten us and the island by now. She'll be at some ball or another dancing with the gentry, mark my word."

Donland turned his attention back to Jackson, "Aye and we will be hip deep in some bog scratching our arses while some smuggler laughs his backsides off."

"Belay that Sir, the admiral will have us and *Hornet* out in the open sea chasing a rich Don for a king's ransom in gold!"

Donland chuckled, "It may well be the Don chasing us; the king of Spain is a jackal lying in the grass waiting to join with France and the rebels. England be hard pressed to fight all three."

The look on Jackson's face soured. "Bloody Dons ain't no more than bloody papists, baby killers!" he said and spat.

Donland was surprised at Jackson's response, he changed tack. "The French have a fleet at Boston."

"Aye, so I've heard, they'll stay put."

"I dare say you are right. Not our concern for I fear when *Hornet* goes to the bottom it will be from rot not shot."

Jackson grinned, "Aye, but before she does, you'll be an admiral."

"A toast before we go," Donland said and lifted his glass, "to bogs, slaves, smugglers and rot!"

"And to you being an admiral!" Jackson answered.

They drank and Donland rose from his chair.

The Spaniard moved to rise but hesitated.

Jackson jerked a chicken leg from the carcass. "Not likely to taste the likes us this for a long while," he said and took a bite while following Donland to the door.

"First stop is the tailor," Donland said. "An acting lieutenant, soon to be a lieutenant, has to have a coat and I need a swab. After that you are to collect as many of the men we came here with as you can find. I will collect David and

Sampson. We will meet on the dock at six bells in the afternoon watch."

Jackson made a mock salute with the chicken leg. "Aye, aye sir!"

Donland found Samson on the street at the door of the inn where the admiral had lodged David. The big Negro came to attention and knuckled his forehead in the navy fashion. He wore ragged brown trousers and a once-white shirt torn in a dozen places. It was the same shirt and trousers he had worn while on the island.

"Is David upstairs?" Donland inquired.

Sampson nodded in reply.

"Wait here," Donland said and entered the building.

David answered the door and stood staring at seeing Donland. "Come in," he managed after a moment.

"You look well David, are you being fed?"

"Aye sir."

"Well gather your belongings you will be going with me. Our admiral has appointed you into my care as a midshipman."

"Aye Sir, I know."

"Then you were waiting for someone to fetch you?"

"Aye Sir."

The boy continued to stand beside the door.

"Fetch your belongings and we'll be off," Donland commanded again.

"I have them Sir," the boy replied.

Donland eyed the youngster, bare-footed and bare-headed. His britches were clean in appearance but with holes in the knees and the shirt without buttons and torn in four places that Donland could see.

"Won't do, no won't do at all," Donland said more to himself than to David. He also considered what remained in his purse. Certainly not enough to outfit the boy in a midshipman's rig, but maybe at least a coat and a hat.

"Let us be off then," he said and then another thought occurred to him, the boy's name.

"Have you a last name?" he asked.

"Yes Sir. Admiral Welles said I should have his name."

Surprised, Donland said, "did he now!"

David looked down at the floor. "He said that since I didn't belong to anyone I should belong to him."

Donland put his hand on the boy's shoulder. "Welles is a fine name. Not many can claim to be named after an admiral."

David looked up, "He said I should tell any who asked that he was my uncle. He said that would help me along the ladder. What does that mean Sir?"

"It means that in His Majesty's service the name will aid you in promotions," Donland said and tousled the boy's hair. "Let us be off."

As Donland closed the door, David said while reaching into his pocket, "I almost forgot, Admiral Welles told me to give you this."

The boy held out a small purse. Donland opened it to find a note, "A small advance on your prize money." Donland beamed, Admiral Welles had advanced a small fortune.

"Let us be away from here Mr. Welles. We must get you outfitted for your duties."

They stopped at one of the tailors on the street that catered to naval officers. He was able to purchase three shirts and three pairs of trousers for David. He ordered a coat and hat befitting a midshipman. He also purchased three swaps for his coats denoting commander. The tailor had nothing in his garments large enough for Samson but promised, after doing the measuring, that he would have two pairs of trousers, two shirts and a sea coat in three days. Two doors down was a cobbler, and he ordered two pairs of shoes for David and a pair for Samson.

The *Hornet* flew the yellow flag of fever both fore and aft. Every boat, ship and skiff in English Harbor knew to give *Hornet* a wide berth. Donland's first attempt to hire a boat to take him to *Hornet* was met with curses. The second even after offering to triple the fee pushed away from the quay without a word. There was nothing for it but to lie and so he did naming the Morgador as the intended destination. In mid harbor he drew his sword and commanded the boat's owner to take him to *Hornet.* The tip of the sword against the man's neck was all the persuasion needed.

There was no movement on deck as they neared *Hornet.* Donland caught sight of one blue coat and was certain his arrival was anticipated but there was no challenge. The boat banged against the hull but no heads appeared above the railing. "Blast their eyes!" he cursed and swung himself onto the ladder. Samson followed at his heels even though the next person should have been David since he was next in rank.

On deck two marines, a midshipman and a scraggy group of half-drunk men lay about. Donland doffed his hat to the quarterdeck. As the others clambered aboard he took from his coat, the order from Admiral Welles and began to read himself in. As he read the midshipman came to attention and kicked one of the marines to do likewise. There was the scruff of hard bare feet, a cough and a sneeze, Donland ignored it all.

"Your name sir?" he addressed the midshipman.

"Aldridge Sir."

"Are you senior here?"

"Aye Sir."

"Very well Mr. Aldridge get this rabble on their feet. Use your dirk if need be."

Aldridge did as ordered, he kicked and threatened and was cursed in return. Even half-drunk the seamen still had enough wits about them to not lay a hand on an officer which was a hanging offense in time of war.

Donland faced the assembled men. He stepped from man to man examining their eyes and then their hands.

Satisfied with what he saw he said, "Mr. Aldridge I'm going below and until I return, you will keep every man here and ready for my command."

"Samson you and David come with me."

Below deck, as his eyes adjusted, he ordered Samson, "Find all the lye soap and any brushes lying about." To David he said, "Find us a lantern, we shall need it."

"A pig's squalor!" Donland said as the lantern light flicked. In the wardroom he found three men in hammocks too sick to rise. Neither was an officer. He took their names and moved on to the captain's cabin and found it in shambles. Turning he made his way to the fore hatch and down to the sail locker and went from there to each storeroom. What he saw was appalling. It would take days to bring order to the disarray he found. To his eye, the former master and his officers were lax in their duties beyond belief. Fever or no, there was no excuse for filth. It was a good thing that Admiral Welles had given him two weeks to prepare to sail. It would at a minimum that amount of time to secure a full complement of men and to set the ship to order.

He discovered rats in the holds and an inch or more of water. Swarms of rats swam to and fro in the bilge which had not been pumped in weeks judging by the amount of water. Thankfully, the hull seemed intact, and he found no rot. The cable locker was a tangle of uncoiled lines and hawsers. Every inch of *Hornet* was in neglect. Paint peeled, the cancer of rust was eating away everything of metal. The deck would take days and a ton of holystone to clean. Jackson would get it all set to rights in due time and Heaven help those who do not do his bidding. It would take all their efforts to set *Hornet* to rights and in fighting order.

The men were assembled as he had left them.

"You six men," Donland called indicating the men standing at the foremast, "Lower a boat." The men looked one to another.

"Now!" Donland shouted. "I'll see your backsides to the gratings if you scum don't move!"

"Reluctantly they did as ordered. Donland's anger did not abate, and he paced as the men lowered the boat.

"Over the side with you." He commanded.

"Sampson, you go into the boat with them and if need be throw them in and the brushes and soap after them."

The big Negro obeyed and followed the men into the boat carrying a bag with brushes and soap.

To the men in the boat he commanded, "Scrub till you bleed and wash every stitch of your filthy rags."

Next Donland pulled a belaying pin from the rack and tossed it down to Sampson. "Use this on any man that isn't clean."

Samson hefted the belaying pin in his massive hand and grinned.

Turning his attention to the remaining crew, "Every man here is going over the side; marines, sick and midshipman. Don't come up until you're clean as the day you come into the world. No one is to go below until I give the order!"

Donland watched as the next six were over the side. He approached the six clean men and inspected each and found them to be reddened but clean. Samson was making good on his assignment.

"Mr. Aldridge!" He called the midshipman.

"Sir!" The boy of about eighteen with dark Spanish features answered.

Donland considered the young man for a moment. He wore a clean shirt and no holes in his clothing. His hat was well worn and ill-fitting.

"How many aboard and how many ashore?"

"Twenty-two aboard sir counting those in the wardroom unfit for duty. Of the others Sir, I do not know. Lieutenant Andrews took eight men and the cutter ashore four days ago." Hesitantly he added, "They left at night."

Donland digested the information. He had a choice; either find Andrews or else mark him as having run. Having the man aboard might prove to be less than desirable if he was of the mindset to run. He would need men he could count on.

"Boat coming Sir!" A seaman announced.

Turning, Donland was pleased to see a cutter containing Lieutenant Jackson and several of the men from the prize crew. These men he knew and could trust.

Sixteen men besides Jackson clamored aboard.

There was no time to waste. "Mr. Jackson put those men with you to make and mend. These others put them to hauling every barrel of water, biscuits and other stones onto deck. Launch the boats if necessary and fill them. I want the holds empty before nightfall."

"Aye Sir." Jackson replied and began barking orders.

"Mr. Aldridge, you will accompany ashore. We'll take the gig so choose your crew."

Donland moved to the railing to observe the washing and to think. There were things he needed to know about *Hornet* and her crew but those things would take time. For the present, he had to set the ship in order and cleaned with lye and lime. In the morning he would inspect all the stores for contamination. With that thought he called, "Mr. Aldridge?"

"Aye Sir!"

"The purser, dead or run?"

"Dead Sir."

"Sailing master?"

"Dead Sir."

"Other midshipmen?"

"Two Sir, both dead."

"Did a surgeon come aboard after the fever was detected?"

"No Sir."

Donland was aware of the men nearby listening. It was not a concern. Every man needed to know that he was in command and was taking charge of their fates. They would learn to trust him. What they did not know and what he suspected was that there was no fever aboard the ship. In his judgment, the men in the wardroom suffered from bad food, rancid and deadly. He would know once he examined the stores. He had seen death from spoiled food when he was a midshipman. The surgeon aboard had called it a bacterium.

That surgeon allowed the young midshipman to peer into what he called a microscope. To Donland's amazement he saw odd shaped and odd colored squiggly things moving in a drop of water. The surgeon explained that most of what was being viewed was harmless but some were deadly. It was when the deadly bacteria multiplied in food or water that men ate or drank that they became sick or died. "Aboard ship every precaution must be taken to ensure the food is free from contaminations" the surgeon has stated on more occasion to the wardroom.

It was almost certain that in this tropical climate that either the food aboard the *Hornet* or the water brought aboard was contaminated. Were it the fever that was killing the men, they would have all perished in a matter of weeks. As it were, some men were not affected and others mildly sick. He had not observed fever in the men in the wardroom. A thorough cleaning of the ship, however, would not come amiss. The stench below made being below unbearable.

CHAPTER TWO

The search for Andrews was short-lived. Donland was told the man was at the inn where David had been housed. Being from a titled family the man was of means. Donland was also told that the lieutenant was most likely drunk and playing cards with another lieutenant.

Andrews answered the knock on the door. His shirt was open, he stunk of dried wine and sweat. He was thin with reddish blond hair, Donland guessed his age at about twenty, maybe twenty-two.

"You are Mr. Andrews?" He asked.

"Aye." The man answered.

"Gather your belonging and be in decent order in ten minutes. We shall wait for you in the street."

Andrews' eyes wandered to the single epaulet on Donland's shoulder. "Commander eh, what ship?"

"*Hornet*!" Donland stated.

Andrews' eyes widened with recognition. "Ten minutes, aye Sir, aye."

The man was true to his word. Andrews, properly attired but unshaved, appeared as requested.

Donland faced the man and stepped closer within inches. He was an inch or two taller than Andrews and able to look slightly down at him. "Sir give me the truth, why were you not aboard managing our people?"

Andrews did not flinch. "It was a living hell. I stayed through the worst of it, not a death in a week."

"That doesn't answer the question. You were senior were you not?"

"Aye Sir, senior for what it was worth."

"You know and I know that you deserted your ship, and those tasked under you. You either broke, or you shrugged off your responsibilities. Neither of which do I countenance as an answer. Your answer or face court-martial?"

Andrews shifted his weight and looked away. The stench of sweat and dried wine were stronger under the heat of the hot sun. When his eyes returned to meet Donland's he said, "Sir, I was drunk and made a stupid decision. It'll not happen again."

"See that it doesn't for I tell you sir that I will not see our people ill-treated nor poorly served. Is that clear?"

"Aye Sir."

"Now, let us buy a pig or two."

"Sir?"

"Pigs, we shall purchase two pigs, fresh fruits and some decent bread for our people. I fear the stores aboard ship are contaminated and are causing the so-called fever. A few good meals should set them to rights."

In addition to the pigs and other foods, Donland purchased two small kegs of wine. He would keep the men from the grog and the water aboard until he could have the casks cleaned and refilled with water he knew to be clean. If he were to meet Admiral Welles deadline of two weeks, he would need every man in the best health possible. He held a suspicion that the two weeks would be shortened considerably if truth be told.

Admiral Welles written orders were not specific. *Hornet* was to be prepared for sea in two weeks with a full complement, stores and cordage. Secrecy he well understood but Admiral Welles had proven himself to withhold information and use misdirection to keep not just enemies off balance but also those who served under him. Using orphans as decoys as he had with young David had proven the man's ability to scheme. The admiral was seldom straight forward and in the days and weeks to come it would do well to remember this fact.

He held little hope of a worthwhile assignment. Even though Admiral Welles wanted *Hornet* fully provisioned and manned, it meant nothing. On this station *Hornet* was far removed from the fleets of Howe and Byron. The great sea fights would be off the coasts of the colonies with the French fleets. English Harbor was far from the war and the opportunities for valor would be few unless the Dons sided with the French and the rebels.

The sun was low in the sky by the time Donland and his party climbed aboard. Jackson was waiting.

The first thing he noticed was that the deck was clear of rubbish, every rope and hawser was coiled or stowed. Men were at work in the crosstrees, others were on their knees with holystones.

"You are making good progress." He said to Jackson.

"Aye Sir."

"Let us get our people fed. I've brought fresh stores for tonight's meal and the morning meal. We shall examine the barrels and other stores tomorrow. They can have all the wine from the casks I've brought aboard. There is also one cask of water, so ration it carefully. No one is to eat or drink of the stores onboard. Is that clear?"

"Aye Sir."

"Have we a cook?"

"I don't know but I do know that Ferguson and Dolan did well for us on the island. With your permission I'll set them to the task."

"Make it so Mr. Jackson."

"Mr. Andrews you will take charge here."

"Aye Sir." Andrews answered.

"Mr. Jackson I will go below with Aldridge to draw up a watch bill. Have David make a list of all the men that came aboard with you and to bring it down to me. Pass the word for Samson to meet me in the captain's cabin."

"Aye Sir."

"Also, you will need to sound the well as I believe we have a leak. The bilge is full and there is water in the holds."

Donland explained to Samson and Aldridge what he wanted done and the three of them set about putting the cabin's cabin in order. Papers and charts were strewn over the deck. They gathered and sorted. The log books were urine stained but mostly legible. The culprits of the mischief would never be caught for they most certainly, according to their messmates, have died of fever.

Samson, even though he was a mute with no tongue, could read and write. He would be a valuable asset in this command.

He watched the big man work. In the colonies the man had been a slave. Fate had brought him and David to *Hornet*. The right and proper thing to do for the big man would be to enter him into the ship's company. If he shared their fate, he should be entitled to rewards that came their way, if any.

"Samson every man aboard has to have a first and last name. On this ship you are a free man and not a slave or servant. I need to enter you into the muster, take the pen and write down your last name. If you don't have one, choose one."

Samson took the pen and in a neat hand wrote Freeman. He looked up at Donland and smiled.

"Freeman it is." Donland agreed and took the pen and entered Samson Freeman into the muster book."

"Now as to your duties aboard this ship, I need a coxswain. A captain's coxswain is primarily in charge of his gig or barge. A coxswain's other duties are to take care of the captain's belongings, bring his meals, and even shave him if asked. Your action station will be by my side at all times and to watch over me in times of danger. Do you understand the gist of what I'm saying?"

In reply, Samson nodded.

"So be it then."

The ship's log was almost impossible to decipher until he came to the years in which the *Hornet* was renamed. The ship was Dutch built for trade with the West Indies colonies. She was captured by the Spanish and sold to a slave trader running slaves from Africa to Brazil. The French seized her, and she was wrecked on a reef rounding Jamaica. An enterprising American merchant had her re-floated and repaired. She continued in the slave trade for another two years but became a derelict when her cargo of slaves and crew died while at sea. She drifted south and was spotted by the sixty-four Yarmouth. A prize crew boarded but quickly abandoned the ship after discovering the decaying corpses. Darkness prevented Yarmouth's captain from sinking the cursed vessel. Admiral Welles upon received the report of the stricken ship detailed a sloop with a prize crew to retrieve her and subsequently refitted and armed giving her the name *Hornet.* That was three months ago. She did seem to be a cursed ship. He wondered how well she would fare under his command. It didn't bear thinking about.

David walked into the cabin while Donland was examining the previous purser's accounts.

Looking up at the boy, he let the beginnings of a smile fade. "No", he thought, "can't show pleasure."

David must have sensed something was amiss for his face contorted into a frown.

"When you report to the captain, it is customary to knock before entering and await the command to enter. Upon entering, you remove your hat and salute. Is that understood?"

The frown upon the boy's face was replaced with surprise. "Aye, Sir" He managed after a moment. Then he remembered to salute.

"You have a lot to learn and very little time to learn it. Therefore, you are to be at Mr. Aldridge's elbow day and night. For no reason are you to leave him. Have you the list I asked for?

"Aye Sir." David answered and produced the list.

Donland took the list and noticed the even neat penmanship.

Mr. Aldridge and Mr. Welles "Report to Mr. Jackson. That is all."

Aldridge replied, "Aye Sir." But David did not move.

"Is there something else Mister Welles?"

"I was wondering about Samson?"

"Samson has been entered into the muster as Samson Freeman, Freeman being a name he chose for himself just as you chose Welles. He will serve as my coxswain. Now be off with you and attend to your duty."

The boy turned to go, Donland commanded, "Stand still."

David turned to face Donland.

"When you are given a command, any command you reply 'Aye, Sir' before you turn to do the captain's bidding. Are you clear on this?"

Solemnly David responded, "Aye Sir."

"Be about your duty Sir." Donland said gently.

"Aye, Sir." David replied and turned for the door.

Discipline was harsh aboard a king's ship, it had to be. Still it was difficult to enforce when there were those you cared for in a ship's company. "For the good of the service", was the mantra of every captain and admiral. Friendship aboard ship was reserved for the lower deck. Duty came before all things and any serving officer who forgot that fact would find himself unemployed. For the good of the service meant duty first; all else was secondary. Every man followed orders whether a lord or a jack, no matter how mundane the order or how heroic. A man's duty was to obey orders.

Donland worked steady for the better part of an hour reading and making notes. He drew a watch bill with the names and duties of the men Aldridge supplied and the list David had prepared. The work was tedious and his mind was on the condition of *Hornet* more so than reading logs and ledgers. The weight of his duties as captain were becoming heavier by the minute as he realized all that he was responsible for. As prize master of the Morgador his duties consisted of sailing the ship, keeping disciple and feeding the men. But as the captain of *Hornet* he would have to keep an accounting of every nail, ball and scrap of food. The purser would do the counting but it would be his responsibility to verify the accounts. The same held true for the master's sail and cordage. It all sat upon his shoulders.

Jackson knocked and entered the cabin.

"Have you secured our cooks?" Donland asked.

"Aye, Captain, our people will be fed within the hour."

"That's good. They will need their strength for what we have before us. I fear there will be no time for idleness. However, we must take care not to over-burden them for we don't yet know the source of the sickness that has plagued the crews?"

Jackson caught what he said immediately, "Crews Captain?"

"Yes, seems that our ship has a rather tragic history. One crew, when she was a slaver, all perished from disease. We must be on our guard and watch for any signs of its reappearance. Our food stores and water must all be examined. I'd rather put it all ashore but I doubt Admiral Welles would approve and replenish our stores. Be vigilant and confide in Mr. Andrews and Mr. Aldridge when you can speak to them each in private."

A tap at the door caused both men to turn.

"Beg pardon sir," Aldridge stammered and entered the cabin. "Brig just entered the harbor under all sail, hoisted, *enemy in sight*! Then *captain repair on board* came up the pole from the admiral. The brig's captain was over the side before the hook was dropped. I thought you should know at once, Sir."

"Thank you Mr. Aldridge."

Jackson and Donland exchanged looks and Donland said to Jackson, "We best go up deck."

An odd-looking fellow was clambering over the side onto the deck as Donland also gained the deck. The newcomer was as filthy and ragged as any man Donland could remember seeing. He saluted the flag and smartly but bare-footed came straight to Donland.

"John Jones, purser Sir."

Donland eyed the man suspiciously; intelligent eyes, smooth hands, and no calluses "Purser you say.

"Aye Sir, Admiral Welles sent me straight over. My orders will come later."

"Straight over? Straight over from where Jones?"

"Prison Sir."

"And your charge?"

"Ah, no charge Sir. Was a bit of a misunderstanding."

"From the looks of you Jones the misunderstanding took some time to sort out."

"Aye Sir, three months and fourteen days." Jones grinned at the statement.

"And this understanding had to do with what exactly?"

"A lady Sir." He winked and drew closer to Donland. In a whisper he said, "Admiral's mistress."

"Stand to Jones!" Donland said vehemently.

Jones came to attention.

Donland did not relax. The man Jones would take liberties if he did. It would not do to extend such liberties for every eye and ear on deck was privy to all that was said and done.

"Do you have dunnage ashore?"

"Aye Sir."

He turned away from Jones and asked Jackson, "Anything?"

"No Sir, gig landed smartly and the brig's captain went straight up to the Admiral's house. Nothing on the pole."

"Very well." Donland answered.

He turned his attention back to Jones, "Fetch your dunnage, back in an hour."

Jones smiled. "Aye Sir."

Something about the tone and the smile unsettled Donland. "My coxswain and a seaman will accompany you to lessen your difficulties."

"Mr. Welles pass the word for Jenkins and Samson."

There was little news during the night. Jones, upon his return, was bathed and dressed in a fresh linen shirt, breeches and shoes with buckles. He did impart to Donland that the brig Shadow was sailing ahead of a Spanish squadron. Admiral Welles would be spending a long night sorting through his options. Spain was not yet at war with England but there was great speculation that she would join the fray. All of England's enemies sensed weakness like a pack of hyenas stalking a weak old lion.

England was far from toothless but the politicos had been having their way and the fleet was greatly reduced in ships and men. The sordid affair with Keppel was just a symptom of the tangle of jealousy and rancor among the senior captains. The bulk of the fleet off the shores of the colonies was reduced to mere transport from the army and patrol. d'Estaing was free to sail and do as he desired as long as he kept his sixteen ships of the line in Boston. But rumor, if it is to believed, was that England had not the ships to equal the French in those waters.

None of that mattered at the moment. *Hornet* was in no shape to aid or hinder anyone. Still flying the flags of fever, she could do nothing but sit and watch the unfolding of events. Until those flags came down, he would use every hour to mold the mixed crew into a ship's company capable of carrying out whatever tasks came their way.

By four bells of the morning watch all hands were busy. Donland, after a breakfast of eggs, biscuits and ham opened the first cask of salt pork that had been swayed out of the hold for inspection. To his dismay it was all dry, ruined. "Over the side with it!" He ordered.

"Mr. Jones enter into your log that the barrel was rotten and disposed of."

"Aye Sir." Jones replied. He wore trousers and shirt of Spanish cut.

Each of the next three barrels was also rotten and disposed of.

Only four of the ten barrels of pork were rotten. The beef was no better, six of twelve. The biscuits were years old, every barrel opened contained almost as many weevils as biscuits.

If was a good thing that the purser was dead, Donland would have hanged him!

The water barrels contained slime.

The ship's stores were far worse than he imagined. It was no wonder men had died and sickness had prevailed. Without proper rations men not only wouldn't work they wouldn't obey either. Mutiny after mutiny had proven the point, but it did not stop greedy pursers and greedy captains from filling the holds of their ships with the cheapest stores that could be bought.

The problem for Donland was how to replace what was thrown over the side. The admiral wouldn't be pleased to see a request for replacement stores. The chandlers and the shops would price their goods according to his desperation. Everything on Antigua had to be brought by ship from England.

CHAPTER THREE

At two bells in the afternoon watch Donland had changed into a clean shirt and breeches. His mind was still working how he would ask Admiral Welles for the necessary stores. And, he was convinced there was no fever aboard the *Hornet* but convincing the admiral may be harder than securing the necessary stores. Jones, the new purser, was very good with figures and had uncovered the treachery of the previous purser. Donland decided the best tack to approach the admiral with would be for Jones to explain the discrepancies in the logs.

Before Donland could summon Jones, Midshipman Welles knocked for admittance.

"Beg Pardon Sir, Mr. Aldridge's compliments, General signal from the Admiral, Captains repair aboard."

"Very well, call away the gig. Mr. Welles we shall attend the admiral."

Six captains were in attendance besides Donland. Seniors were Okes from *Medusa*, Hotham from Preston and Griffith from Conqueror. The other three were commanders of small brigs. Admiral Welles looked as if he were awake all night.

"The news in the air is that Spain is about to oppose us and join with the revolutionaries and the French. I can only tell you that if Spain comes to war, then only God can save us." Welles all but wrung his hands.

"But what of Admiral Hyde Parker?" Griffith asked.

"He is cruising east of Martinique waiting for d'Estaing's arrival. We have reports that he has sailed from off Boston. But if the Spanish squadron joins d'Estaing, then I fear Hyde Parker will be over-matched. Therefore we must make ready to assist and to give warning."

"How so Sir?" Hotham asked.

"I'm sure the French will endeavor to recapture the islands they lost last year. When the fight comes, it will be somewhere to our south. We will therefore deploy scouting vessels in a line as far south as Martinique. Also, I will send *Hornet* with dispatches for Admiral Hyde Parker."

"But the fever Sir?" Hotham asked.

"Ah, there are no new cases that I'm aware. Mr. Donland is that so?"

"No sir and I have examined the ship's stores and found them most foul. It appears the sickness was caused by bad food."

"There, satisfied Captain Hotham?"

"If Captain Donland is satisfied Sir."

For a moment Donland wasn't quite sure how to answer. It was the first time a senior officer had referred to as captain. It literally took his breath away."

"Yes Sir, I am quite satisfied and will bear responsibility for my claims."

"Good, good, gentleman. Let us get on with the other details." Welles said.

Donland heard the six bells of the afternoon watch, so did Admiral Welles who straightened from the chart table,

"Gentlemen, I will send across your orders before the tide in the morning."

Donland waited until all have retrieved their hats and were conversing. "Admiral Welles, Sir?"

"Yes what is it?" Welles snapped.

Donland was aware of the older man's weariness and did not take affront. "As I said, the stores aboard *Hornet* are fouled, what remains is not enough for even a short cruise. I..."

Welles cut him short. "Plenty of stores on that frigate you brought in?"

"Aye Sir." Donland managed.

"There's your answer then. Fetch what you need be it stores or whatever. Just be ready to sail when my orders get to you." Welles scooped up a chart and quickly disappeared into his private room.

"To Morgador!" Donland ordered as he stepped into the gig. "There's not a moment to lose."

If he was to fill his holds and complement his command with more men, Morgador was his best option. It would also be in the minds of the other captains. He had to get there first and take off anything and anyone he could use. Each captain would know full well that if the Spanish were to declare war of England then the likelihood of every ship of his majesty's navy would be at sea for a very long time.

"Back to *Hornet* lads and be double quick about it. Send my compliments to Lieutenant Jackson to send across all boats. He is to have Mr. Andrews set the other men to scouring the holds and cleaning every available water cask."

Putting his foot on the first rung of the ladder he called back, my compliments to Mr. Welles to come across with the muster book."

He didn't look back as he climbed through the sally port. A midshipman he didn't know approached. The young man saluted and state, "Midshipman Kinley Sir."

"Mr. Kinley who is in command?"

"I am Sir. Acting Lieutenant and commander."

"Well very Mr. Kinley. The Admiral has instructed me to take away any stores, cordage and men that I find suitable."

Shock registered on the youngster's face. He appeared to Donland about to object but then discipline stilled him. "Aye Sir." came weakly.

"How many aboard?" Sixteen seaman, another eight wounded or ill and forty-four prisoners."

"Forty-four!" Donland exclaimed.

"Aye Sir, eight French, three Spaniards and the rest slaves."

Donland frowned. He had hoped to gain ten or more men but evidently the other captains had selected the prime hands before the admiral's meeting. He would be hard pressed to put to sea with so few men.

"Very well, have them all on deck and under guard. I shall go below and examined the stores."

The holds were as he had remembered. There were ample stores, mostly French but the English seaman's bellies wouldn't know the difference. He counted barrels of pork, beef and biscuits. There were also casks filled with dried fruits, these would be a welcome addition.

Gaining the deck once again, Donland waited as the shackled prisoners were arraigned on deck. The French and Spaniards he couldn't trust. The Negroes stood silent in their rags and chains. These would not be his concern but he had in his mind that one or two might be seaman from a slaver.

"Where did this lot come from?" Donland asked Kinley.

"Slave ship sir, making the run for Africa I was told."

"Not from Africa?"

Again the questioning look on the young man's face. "Aye sir."

A boat bounced alongside. Donland turned and waiting to see who would be clambering up the side. He hoped it would be his men and not some other Captain more senior to himself.

To his delight, the first man was Samson. The big man came straight to him and knuckled his forehead as he often did when coming face to face with Donland.

"Samson examine these men, take your time. Determine which may suitable to join our ship's company."

Samson was a head taller than every man on deck. He could not speak but his sheer size intimidated those in shackles. He walked among them, examined them from both front and back. Occasionally he would put his finger on what appeared to be a scar on a man's body.

Samson returned to Donland. Holding up his hands he signaled twenty-eight.

"Twenty-eight men?" Donland asked.

Samson knuckled his forehead.

"Very well then." He said more to himself than to anyone as he approached the men. Standing in front of them, he said "I need a man who speaks English. Raise a hand if you do."

Four hands went up. Then with hesitation three more."

He pointed to one of the last three, "What is your name?"

"Its Bill sir, no last name just Bill."

"Bill how is it that you are among these slaves."

"I too am a slave sir. Born a slave and raised in Jamaica. I and these men all slaves, we crew ship for Senior Guerrero. He blackbirder."

What Bill said confirmed his suspicion that one of the French or Spanish was the owner of the captured slave ship and he used slaves as the crew. It was not an uncommon practice, cheaper by far than paying a crew. Guerrero was probably not the owner but the captain and the other men would be the paid guards during the voyage.

Donland said to the shackled men "Any man among you that would be free and willing to serve aboard my ship is asked to make his mark. You will serve as free men, not slaves and earn the King's shillings."

The men exchanged astonished looks.

"Sir you can't do that!" Kinley exclaimed. "These men are the King's property; they are to be sold at auction."

Donland turned to face the young man. "Aye the king's property they are and the king's property they will remain as are you and I."

"Mr. Welles?"

"Aye Sir." David said as he came forward to Donland.

"You will ask each man his name and ask if he speaks English. If he can answer and speaks English, Samson will record his name in the book, today's date, nation of origin and have the man sign it or make his mark."

"Aye Sir." David answered.

"Samson you will assist Mr. Welles.

"Dawkins set our men to bringing up stores from the holds; twenty barrels of pork, twenty of beef, eighteen barrels of biscuits and all the barrels of dried fruit."

"Aye Sir." Dawkins answered and began called men forward for their tasks.

Clouds filled the sky mid-afternoon. The tropical rains swept the harbor cooling the men as they labored with the barrels. Donland's watchfulness of their efforts was interrupted when a boat came alongside and deposited a rotund middle-aged man by the name of Fredricks and a taller lanky man in his mid-thirties whose name was Malcolm Dewitt. The older man was in his cups with what appeared to be vomit on his coat lapels.

"Doctor Fredricks Sir, as ordered." The man stated flatly.

Donland was certain the man did not wish to be aboard. "Surgeon?" He asked.

"That would be correct. May I go below Sir?"

"Do you have orders Doctor Fredricks?" Donland inquired.

The man was already moving toward the hatch and said over his shoulder. "Be along shortly."

Donland stood stunned for a moment and then realized there were men watching. Mr. Aldridge see to the surgeon and be quick about it!"

Before Aldridge reached the hatchway Fredricks head appeared. "By whose orders where those fever flags removed?"

"Mine!" Donland snapped back.

Fredricks head disappeared once more.

Dewitt stood as a silent witness to the proceedings. Donland had forgotten the man.

"Sailing master Sir." Dewitt said as he thrust forward his papers.

Donland took them, examined them and then asked, "New York?"

The man's eyes twinkled, "New London Sir, and you?"

"Salem and later New York."

Dewitt was about to extend his hand but thought better of it. Donland smiled at the gesture.

"Know these coasts?" Donland asked.

"Aye Sir, as well as I knows the Banks."

"Whig or Tory?"

"Neither Sir, king's man only."

"Very well then we shall have no difficulties."

"Aye Sir." Dewitt said and then stated, "Beg Pardon Sir but you are a mite young for a commander."

Rather than berate the man Donland said, "Age may have privileges, but the prize goes to the bold."

Dewitt nodded in understanding. Donland's command of *Hornet* had not come with privilege but was earned.

The first order Donland had given once coming from Morgador was to order the fever flags removed. It mattered not to him that no surgeon had given the order. He had seen no evidence of fever and the sooner those flags were down then the sooner the men aboard would be at ease.

Jackson was as busy as a one-armed weaver. He was from one group of men to the next commanding in the sharpest tones Donland had ever heard the good-natured man use. He was leaving no doubt in their minds as to who was the first lieutenant and they had better damn well follow his orders. "The cat is in the bag but it can be across your backs if you don't jump too!" he shouted on several occasions. The men jumped.

The tasks of putting the ship to rights and stowing the stores went smoothly, considering the assortment of men. They seemed to sense that this ship was to be different that others they had served. Donland wanted them to feel that way, he would be like Captain Oakes in that he would be fair but heaven help the slackers. He would require every man to do his duty and to do it gladly. Should any man abuse another then that man would be sternly dealt with. This would be true for his officers as well, but as yet he had seen no evidence that any of them were tempered to be abusive. He watched, observed but did not interfere as the men labored. He forced himself to remain apart and to hold his tongue.

To his amazement the men fell into a rhythm as if they had served together for a long period. The former slaves from the slave ship surprised him at their skill and seamanship. They went about their work and every task assigned to them with a smile and Donland attributed that to the fact that they were not being forced or threatened with whips. They were free men who valued their new found freedom even if it were aboard a King's ship.

The Admiral's orders arrived before sunset. To Donland's great relief he had thirty-six hours to finish his preparations for sailing, to secure cordage and stores and to sort out his ship's company. He believed he had sufficient time for the men to settle in and become familiar with their messmates. By the dawning of the third day they should be able to function as one company. However, he held no high hopes as to their ability with the guns. They may do well with sail but he was under no illusions as to their performance in a fight. Exercising the guns would be his top priority aside from a timely passage. According to the Admiral's orders he could expect no help on the voyage, as there would be no friendly ships between Antigua and Martinique. Every and any encounter would be best viewed as a threat. He was reminded that England's enemies were many. *Hornet* was to make a quick passage and return with all haste. Welles had stated, "No prizes even if the buggers want to surrender! Speed is of the essence!"

Upon hearing their destination and their assignment Jackson had grinned and said, "Not up to our arses in a bog!"

Midmorning of his second day Jackson was summoned aboard the flagship. He scrambled about to find a suitable uniform. Between Donland and Aldridge they managed to turn him out in a decent rig. Jackson rejected the fuss but Donland assured him that standing before a board of captains was not entirely about seamanship. "These men are officers and gentlemen and to be admitted to their ranks you must show yourself to be of the same cloth." Jackson's face had paled at that.

Donland continued, "There will be at least four post captains. You will probably be the last to be examined as protocol dictates that those put forth by the admiral and those of peerage get first dibs. I've heard there will be four of you to be examined, Kinley, the admiral's nephew and two others from the ships in harbor. The captains will have exhausted their brandy and their patience by the time you are called. Your knowledge of ship and sail plus your navigation skills should get you past most questions. As to your leadership qualities, you know how to lead men. Be honest and straightforward; do not hedge. Uncertainty is the weakness they will be looking for."

Jackson did not return until the forenoon watch was called. He came aboard in the rig of a newly commissioned lieutenant. Hat, coat, shirt and neckerchief were still crisp despite the heat. A sword was clipped to his waist.

"Come below Mr. Jackson," Donland ordered.

"Aye, aye Sir," Jackson replied as straight faced as standing before a court of inquiry.

"Samson bring us a bottle of wine and three glasses not pots."

"I take it you spent all your prize money?" Donland asked.

"A good sum of it, yes. The tailor was a foul fellow, and he knew my haste and it cost me dearly. The same for the chandler selling me the sword," Jackson explained and drew the sword. "It's a fair blade."

Donland received the sword and examined it. "Appears to be good steel, a bit heavy for my taste."

Samson poured wine in two glasses.

"Fill the third Samson."

Samson did so.

Donland handed the first glass to Jackson and the second to Samson. "I'm sure you have no qualm with Samson joining our toast? But for him and his service on the island neither you nor I would be here to drink this bottle."

"Well said Sir," Jackson answered.

Donland lifted his glass, "To Lieutenant Jackson, may this be the first of many promotions in the King's service."

"Aye!" Jackson agreed.

Samson, as was his custom, knuckled a salute.

Jackson picked up the bottle and filled their glasses. "Another Sir, to *Hornet*."

To Donland's surprise, Samson took the bottle and filled each glass. He pointed to Donland and then to Jackson and grunted. They lifted their glasses and drank.

"It's time to be about our duties," Donland said.

"Mr. Jackson we have a surgeon come aboard, a fellow by the name of Fredricks. He did not present himself and gave me no orders. Pass the word for him to report to me."

"Aye Sir," Jackson acknowledged then asked, "Queer fellow is he?"

"I believe so. Either the admiral wanted rid of him or he has some other purpose than surgeon to be among us."

"In that case, I shall fetch him personally," Jackson said with a grin.

Jackson appeared several minutes later. Fredricks had evidently brought a personal store of liquor aboard in his personal dunnage. The man was having difficulty standing.

"Doctor Fredricks are you to join this company or be a passenger?" Donland put it bluntly to the drunken man.

"Passenger; nothing more," Fredricks managed.

"Where is his dunnage Mr. Jackson?"

"Midshipman's berth Sir."

"Samson!" Donland barked.

"Convey Doctor Fredricks and his dunnage to Mr. Jackson's cabin. If he is to be a passenger, then we shall accommodate him."

Samson evidently had experience with conveying drunken men. He grasped Fredricks by the arm and guided the man from the cabin.

"Mr. Jackson send Mr. Andrews across and instruct him make inquires of the admiral's staff. I should like to know more of Doctor Fredricks before we sail."

CHAPTER FOUR

Andrews knocked at the cabin door two hours later. He brought with him a packet from the admiral. "You better read this before I report on what I learned," Andrews said as he handed Donland the packet.

There were three letters in the packet aside from the official packet intended for Admiral Hyde-Parker, the first addressed to Donland from Admiral Welles and he was instructed to give passage to Doctor Herman Fredricks to the squadron off Martinique. Further he was to keep the man sober until he was discharged from *Hornet*. Should there be a need for the surgeon's services Fredricks was required to do as bidden. *Hornet* was to make a fast passage and return as swiftly as possible. Welles made it clear that there were to be no delays, not for prizes or curiosity. Speed was a quality not to be wasted.

"And what news have you Mr. Andrews?"

Andrews didn't hesitate. "Doctor Fredricks is a notorious drunkard but a capable surgeon when sober. He is very fond of the young women of Antigua. He's not a gambler."

"He is to be a passenger Mr. Aldridge therefore once we remove his supply of spirits he should give us no trouble. We have no women aboard." Donland's eyes widened, and he asked, "Or do we?"

"Not at present Sir. Mr. Jackson had them sent ashore earlier today." Andrews answered and smiled.

Donland matched his smile. "Now Mr. Andrews what is it you haven't told me?"

"Sir?"

"Mr. Andrews I've reported to a few captains in my time and in the course of my years I learned what to share with my captain and what not to share. My suspicion is that you obtained information about the surgeon that is somewhat more derogatory than what you have reported. Even gossip has some merit if accepted as such. Therefore, tell me what you have heard and what you suspect. What you have to say is for my ears only. If there is a threat to this ship and her company, I need to know before it materializes."

Andrews blew a breath. "I was told that Doctor Fredricks was violent toward several of the island women and one officer's wife in particular. Admiral Welles is getting rid Fredricks before the officer returns. By all accounts Fredricks is a vicious and violent man not to be trusted around any woman. I was also told that the man will do almost anything for money including committing murder for a fee."

Donland moved to behind his desk and sat in his chair. "Seems the man will have to be watched, can't allow him an opportunity to cause of hardship. That will be all Mr. Andrews."

"Samson!" Donland called.

When Samson entered he motioned for him to come close. He was well aware of listening ears in a small command such as *Hornet.* The marine sentries at his cabin door heard most conversations in the cabin and there were always men on deck will acute hearing.

Samson came within arm's length and Donland motioned him closer still. "The surgeon in Mr. Jackson's cabin needs watching during this passage. Assist him as you may, stay close and keep the man from mischief. When he goes to the head you will locate his spirits and pour them over the side. I will manage here."

Their first day out of the harbor was uneventful. With a good wind from the starboard quarter they adjusted the trim to gain better sailing qualities of the *Hornet.* The men were evaluated and assigned watches that made the best use of their particular skills and demeanor. Donland had discovered the trick when he was a midshipman and could never understand why captains neglected setting men into watches based on both their skills and their personal interactions. Of Fredricks he saw him only once as the man made for the head. Jackson dealt with the man's outburst when he discovered his store of spirits was missing. Samson intimidated the man to silence and sleep.

The former slaves were simply astonishing. They were quick and angle. Donland watched them as they worked aloft and seemed as free as birds amongst the rigging. Signing them into the muster book, he concluded, was a stroke of good fortune. He only hoped they would fight when the fight would come.

A three-quarter moon hung above *Hornet* as she glided along on a calm sea. Scattered clouds with edges of silver floated to the west like ghost ships. The ship's wake sparked in the moonlight. Donland was not at peace and he told himself that he should be. He had his first command, and he had men serving with him that he could trust, some he called friends. His career was made as long as he kept his wits about him. God had blessed him in many ways, so why was he feeling melancholy? The men working above and beyond him spoke in whispers not wanting to disturb their captain who stood aft of the helm. To all intents he was alone standing there in the moonlight with the wind upon his cheek.

Her face came to him as clear as the bright moon. It was such a night as this that he had kissed her. Betty Sumerford was in Boston thousands of miles to his north. Her note stated that she could not compete with his first love and would not be his mistress. She had seen more clearly than he that the ship that he served would always be first in his life. What she had written was that she had given up love in order to have a chance at happiness. But what of the man she loved, now captain of his own ship? Would the love that was denied him forever burn in his heart? Would there be another?

He considered the captains that he knew and questioned how they were able to be committed to a woman and a ship. How was it possible to love both deeply and separately given all that each required? Were they not distracted by loneliness? Did they long for the land while at sea and long for sea while on land? Was heartache a constant companion no matter where he was? He pondered these questions while he heard every sound of his ship and felt the slightest of changes of the wind.

The bell struck six times signaling the nearing of the first watch. Jackson would be relieving Andrews in an hour and then the two midshipmen Aldridge and young David would share a watch. Dewitt would come up in the forenoon.

Being captain and mentor to the young gentlemen was something he had not considered before taking command of *Hornet.* But it was the navy way and the well-being, training and education of these young gentlemen was his responsibility as was the care of every man aboard. The burden of command was growing heavy in this late hour. It would be midnight soon and he should put this day behind him for the morning may bring challenges.

Samson prepared a breakfast of eggs, ham and ship's biscuit. He also set out a pot of grape jam. Donland ate as if it were his last meal. He was just finishing the third of the five biscuits on the plate when a knock sounded. "Enter!" he called as he swallowed.

David Welles, tan and taller than Donland remembered removed his hat. The scar ran almost the width of his forehead just below his hairline. It was an ugly thing and the boy would have died from the wound had it not been for Samson.

"Mr. Jackson's compliments Sir, a sail is sighted to the east. He said there is no hurry as he thinks it is a single sail luger of sorts."

Donland noticed the boy's eyes on the jam pot. "I shall go up and I would not take it amiss if there are no biscuits on the plate when I return."

"Mr. Dewitt says she is a trader making for Portsmouth," Jackson stated

"No doubt they will inform the French of our course." Donland said.

"Aye Sir."

Donland studied the sails and the wind for a moment. "We'll continue this heading as long as the wind is favorable. I shouldn't think the French will come after us. We've too much sea room and too much distance for anything afloat to catch up to us. We should sight our ships before nightfall."

Just after five bells in the afternoon watch the masthead hailed the deck, "Sail two points on the larboard!" By the time Donland gained the deck the lookout reported three additional ships.

"Ship of the line! Two fourth rates! Fifth rate changing tack!" the Lookout called.

"I suspect they have spotted us and will be sending someone to investigate. Run out the colors and make our number," Donland said Jackson.

As if the commander of the squadron had heard him the lookout called down, "Ship changing tack!"

Aldridge, Welles and Andrews were on deck as were the purser Jones and Dewitt. There were not enough telescopes to go around, so they were sharing two of the smaller ones. All were relieved to see the ensign hoisted on the approaching ship.

"Thetis Sir, thirty-two guns, Captain Blankett!" Andrews informed Donland.

Donland saw the signal go up before Andrews informed him of the message, "Heave to!" It made no sense, but it was an order. "Reduce sail Mr. Jackson and heave to."

A boat was lowered from the Thetis before the way came off of *Hornet*. Donland put the telescope to his eye and saw a midshipman was in charge of the boat. "Something is amiss," he said more to himself than to anyone on deck.

The midshipman, a boy of sixteen or so called up from the boat when it neared, "Captain Blankett's compliments Sir. He asks your name and your mission?"

Aldridge said, "Curious" and instantly regretted it as Donland turned to face him. "Stand to!" Donland barked.

The deck was a hush except for the wind in the rigging.

"I am Commander Donland. We have dispatches for Admiral Hyde-Parker from Antigua."

"If you please Sir, Captain Blankett has instructed me to receive your dispatches."

Donland turned and called, "Mr. Dewitt a word."

Dewitt left his station beside the chart table and came to Donland.

In a whisper Donland asked, "Can you identify those ships?"

"Aye Sir and I've met the young gentleman, Snipes is his name."

Donland rubbed his chin and asked, "All is as it appears?"

Dewitt replied, "Aye Sir. I see no hint of treachery. All the captains and even Admiral Hyde-Parker would know *Hornet*'s troubles. I would venture they are being cautious of a fever ship."

Donland nodded, "Aye, it would seem so."

He turned from Dewitt and peered down at Midshipman Snipes. "My compliments to Captain Blanklett, tell him that we are clear of fever and will stand off if it pleases him."

"Samson fetch the dispatches," he commanded.

Samson returned in minutes and handed the dispatches to Donland.

"Mr. Snipes do not fumble the packet into the sea! Are you ready?" Donland asked.

"Aye Sir," the boy answered.

Donland tossed the packet and Snipes caught it with both hands.

"Out oars," Snipes commanded, and they pushed away from *Hornet.*

Donland yelled to Snipes, "Avast there Mister Snipes."

Snipes paid no heed so Donland said, "Lord Hyde-Parker's surgeon, Doctor Fredricks is aboard and is to be taken off."

Snipes turned and faced Donland, "I will inform Captain Blankett Sir!"

"Also inform him that Admiral Welles has requested that *Hornet* return with all haste."

"Aye Sir," Snipes called back.

Hornet lay off Thetis' larboard beam for the night. At noon she was ordered by signal to the lee of Suffolk. There was no communication between *Hornet* and the other ship's other than the signals. Donland felt like a red-haired stepchild. The next morning a boat was lowered and pulled to

Hornet. A lieutenant sat in the stern sheets, he did not come aboard.

"Admiral Rowley's compliments Commander. I'm flag lieutenant Lassiter and have orders from Admiral Rowley. Lower a line and I will pass them to you."

Donland's anger had been smoldering during the long wait and the lack of courtesy. "This is most irregular," he complained.

Lassiter was indignant, "These are my orders from the admiral."

"What of the surgeon Fredricks?" Donland asked.

"Keep him!" Lassiter answered.

Donland accepted the slight and liked none of it. "Very well we shall get under way."

Turning he saw Dawkins, "Dawkins throw a line to the boat and pull it up when the packet is tied on."

When the packet cleared the railing Donland turned to Jackson, "Get us under way Mr. Jackson. Let us be clear of these waters and the stench!"

His orders were a scrawled sentence with Admiral Rowley signature, "Return to Antigua." There were no dispatches to be delivered to Admiral Welles. Most unusual!

It was Dewitt who came to Donland's cabin later to explain. "Admiral Hyde-Parker is like Cornwallis, neither trusts anyone born in the colonies. He would not trust you with dispatches unless you were born on the Tames. I've experienced the same mistrust on more than one occasion and that's why, when we met I was bold enough to ask where you were from."

Donland nodded in understanding. As second lieutenant in a frigate where he was born wasn't of consequence. As a commander, his loyalty could be questioned. "Thank you Mr. Dewitt," he said.

Dewitt turned to go and Donland asked, "And what of you, sailing master on a sloop at your age?"

Dewitt stopped and turned. "You may as well know, the misadventures of youth were my undoing. Being the third son of a prominent New London family, I was sent to the navy to make my career. Was acting lieutenant in the old Shrewsbury about to take my examination but two nights before sitting for the board I drank too much and gambled too much. Then I talked too much. It was the talking that was my undoing. Sniveling toff reported me for saying that it was high time the royals did honest work and got their heels off the necks of working men. Of course, coming from an American it amounted to treason. The board rejected me and I was discharged in fifty-one. Father died and the creditors took everything my older brother didn't gamble away. Signed on under the name of Dewitt in fifty-two as master's mate in a merchantman. Got my ticket in fifty-nine."

"I'm sure there is more color to the story," Donland replied with a grin.

"Aye Sir, but I'll not tell it."

They studied one another for a long second then Dewitt asked, "Lieutenant Jackson; he's junior to the other?"

"Aye, he is. Rear-Admiral Welles made the appointment. At the time it was not known if there were any lieutenants still aboard. The fever took most of the crew."

"But seniority Sir."

"Loyalty first Mr. Dewitt, loyalty first. I believe that was the admiral's intent.

Dewitt grinned, "I would venture to say that was also in the admiral's mind in choosing you for command."

Donland was taken aback. He had not considered the admiral's point of view. The admiral could use him as a pawn in any game he chose. "I see your point Mr. Dewitt; I owe my station to him."

"As do I," Dewitt said.

"For the good of the service," Donland stated and grinned.

Their conversation was interrupted by a light tapping on the door.

"Enter!" Donland ordered.

Andrews stood in the doorway, "Mr. Jackson's compliments sir. He requests you come on deck."

"My compliments to the first lieutenant, I shall be up shortly. And, my compliments to Doctor Fredricks, inform him that he will be returning to Antigua."

CHAPTER FIVE

The topsails of the squadron had disappeared over the horizon. The sky was clear except for a light haze of high thin clouds. Donland gauged the wind as fitful coming from northeast.

"We'll lose steerage soon," Dewitt said behind Donland.

"Aye," Jackson added. "Perhaps we should tack to larboard?" he suggested to Donland.

"What say you Mr. Dewitt?" Donland asked.

"Starboard sir, current is running about two knots, we need to get outside of it and pick up a stronger westerly. If we don't we'll be becalmed in an hour and drifting with that current."

"Very well gentlemen. It will mean more sea miles to Antigua but better more miles than drifting back to Rowley."

In unison Jackson and Dewitt replied, "Aye!"

"Mr. Jackson, you and Mr. Dewitt will join me tonight for supper. There are a few matters we need to discuss," Donland said to them. "I will go below."

Donland was apprehensive about the evening meal. It would be his first with those under his command. He chose

Dewitt and Jackson and not the lieutenants because these were the two men he would rely upon the most during this command. Their ages and their experiences would help guide many of his decisions. He well remembered the burden of command as he fulfilled his orders to sail the damaged Morgador to Antigua. Many regarded the actions that took place and the subsequent prizes to be luck but he knew better. Experienced men such as Jackson had guided decisions, seen faults in his plans and suggested caution at the appropriate times. Command was his and the consequences of all decisions rested upon him. Yes, he possessed a gift of sorts to read men and know their motives but Dewitt and Jackson had years of practical experience and knowledge beyond his own.

Samson prepared roast pork smothered in onions and peppers on a bed of rice, yams, a bean soup, and an apple pudding. The small cabin was the envy of every man on deck. Their usual fare of salt beef or pork, ship's biscuits and water paled in comparison to the captain's table. To compensate the men he ordered a ration of dried fruit for each man. He dared not allow them fruit too often, as they tended to store it to make liquor.

The table conversation between the three was limited to sailing and a smattering of personal history. Dewitt talked at length of winds, currents and hurricanes. Jackson retold the crash of the French frigate that he had lured away from Morgador.

The last of the meal was consumed and Samson brought in a bottle of brandy. Donland had saved it when he captured the Aimee. It was one of the few things left to remind him of the treachery of bloody Mr. Howard.

"To King George!" Donland toasted.

They drank and were silent. Donland was aware that in their brief time together aboard *Hornet* that the two men sitting at his table had learned to read him as easily as he read them. They would not waste time with frivolous toasts.

"We are war and our enemies are numerous," Donland stated. "Because our enemies are numerous, there is a great amount of distrust among even our allies. The distrust extends even to the loyal men of our service. This morning we had a taste of that and it has left a vile lingering odor that no amount of brandy is going to remove. The reason that I have invited you to share a meal with me is that we may lay before each other our beliefs and our loyalties. Each of us must depend upon the other and should there be areas of conflict we need to know where those are before we face an enemy. Since ours is a small company, greater must be our trust of one another."

Donland looked into Dewitt's eyes, "Mister Dewitt when you came aboard it was evident to me that you questioned my leadership ability because of my age. I did not take that amiss nor do I feel threatened by you. I am sure that you have heard of how Mister Jackson and I were given command of the prize frigate Morgador and of the difficulties we encountered. Some things that you may have heard are exaggerated, but that is neither here nor there. What you need to understand is that it was a task that was completed, there was a loss of life, there was treason and treachery and there were many heroic efforts on the behalf of those who served me.

Mister Jackson was justly rewarded for his service, for his duty and for the heroic efforts to save not only the ship but the company. He has earned his step many times over. He is a man I trust not only with my life and also with this ship. I owe this man a great debt and all I have to offer him is my friendship."

Mister Dewitt I perceive that you are a like-minded man as myself. That you just as I, believe that justice is important no matter a man's station in life. And to that end you would seek to unto injustice if it were within your power. Is that so?"

Cautiously Dewitt answered, "aye captain."

Donland continued, "having said all of this, I would like for each of you to know that I hold no political views and that I will not tolerate the conveying of any political views while serving on this vessel. Though I am born in America my loyalty is to King George, to England and to the Navy. Should the colonies win freedom from the crown my loyalty will still be to the crown. The reason for this is that I wear the King's coat and as long as I wear his coat and receive his shilling I will be the King's man.

My purpose for telling you these things is that you will have no doubt as to my loyalty. Now I must ask you, what of your loyalty?"

Beyond the bulkhead they could hear the sound of a fiddle, men's laughter and raised voices as men played cards. Above them were the sounds of a working ship at sea. But in the small cabin there was silence.

Donland waited for one of the two men to speak but both only stared into their glasses. He sighed heavily and said, "The silence is deafening gentleman. I'm waiting."

At that both men looked up, each met the others eyes.

"I know no life but this life," Jackson stated. His eyes met Donland's. "You have saved my life, and I have saved yours, thus we are bound together. I will follow your orders not only because you are my captain but because I am in your debt." He paused and then continued, "I will follow your orders because you are my captain to whom I owe loyalty. I will stand against all who oppose you and I will stand with you when others do not." Having said that, he lifted his glass, remembered that it was empty and reached for the bottle.

Dewitt leaned back in his chair and crossed his legs. He stretched and put his hands behind his head. He looked across the table to Jackson and then to Donland. "Gentleman I owe no man loyalty, certainly not any of those making war against England or seeking freedom from England. Nor do I owe the enemies of England anything. Mister Jackson said that he would follow your orders because of a debt that he owes but I owe no such debt. But I will say this, you are the captain of this ship and when I signed aboard, I bound myself to your orders. In the short time that I have served aboard the ship, I have observed that respect is not forced but is given as received. It is it not a matter of uniforms nor of authority but rather the worth of the man. The invitation to this meal was another mark of respect, not one that I earned but one that is given simply because I am a man. I am not a thing to be commanded and certainly not abused. Yes, captain I will obey your orders and I will do so because you have shown respect for me as a man and as a man of worth."

Donland nodded, "Well said Mr. Dewitt." He paused then continued, "Gentlemen we do not know what enemies we shall face nor from what quarter shall they come. Neither of us comes from peerage nor do we have wealth, all we have is this ship and each other. I will, as Mister Dewitt has said, give respect to any man due respect and I will also defend any man of this ship's company against those who abuse them or accuse them unjustly. I ask the same of you."

He took a sip from his glass, "This ship has a bad mark against it, namely the fever. Mr. Dewitt and I have marks against us in that we were born to colonist families. There will be those who will make decisions about us based on those marks. We may be abused and misused by them but we are powerless against them for they have rank, peerage and influence. We have no choice but to sail together and to fight together. This ship is to be our world and this company our people," he paused then asked, "What say you?"

"Aye!" Jackson said with seriousness etched on his face.

"Aye Sir!" Dewitt answered. "And well said sir."

"Let us drink to *Hornet*, to respect, duty and to loyalty!" Donland said as he filled the glasses.

"To *Hornet*!" he said while raising his glass.

"To *Hornet*!" they replied.

Hornet found the wind four hours later after several tacks and shifting of sails. Donland had left that task to Dewitt and Jackson. His pressing concern was the report he was drafting for Admiral Welles. What he said and how he said was to be a balance of tact and fact. Jealousy among senior officers was well known in the service and in government. Keppel, Byng and Rodney were all of the same cloth as far as he was concerned. So, what he put to paper for the remainder of his career would be sifted with caution. Again, the weight of command weighted upon him. Every decision he would make would no longer be scrutinized by his captain but by an admiral and those of the admiralty. Mistakes in judgment and weakness of command would be noted in some journal and referenced as promotion is considered or new posting are made available. His career was placed in jeopardy with every report he wrote and the careers of those who served under him could likewise suffer. He could never write what was in his mind but could set down only events as observed from afar. That would be the safest course. He had learned that bit of wisdom when being questioned by Admiral Welles on the details of delivering Morgador.

English Harbor was alive with ships and bumboats plying the waters the morning *Hornet* dropped her hook. The sun was hot, and every man glistened with sweat. They were again lying to the far side of the harbor as when flying the fever flag. "Captain repair aboard!" had run up the pole of the admiralty before *Hornet* was half way across the harbor. Donland had his reports ready, Samson had washed and pressed the uniform, all he had to do was dress. He was certain that the flag lieutenant Duncan would meet him. The man still was an irritation.

Duncan was not present. Flag Lieutenant Coutts introduced himself and said, "Vice-Admiral Welles has been dispatched to Savannah. Captain Yorke will receive your dispatches and reports. You are to return to your ship and prepare to carry dispatches to Savannah. You will report to the Flagship of Vice-Admiral Arbuthnot. Your sailing orders and the Admiral's dispatches will be sent to you before you sail on the tide tomorrow. If there are questions concerning your reports you will be called."

Donland asked, "What of the Surgeon Fredricks? Admiral Rowley refused him."

"Do you have a surgeon aboard other than Doctor Fredricks?"

"No."

Coutts grinned, "Well sir, I suggest you keep him."

Donland sat in the stern sheets fuming over his treatment. The gossip that boiled throughout Antigua and the West Indies fleet about himself and *Hornet* must be considerable. He had done nothing but his duty yet jealousy of was poisoning even that. And to add insult to injury he still had Fredricks.

"We sail on the tide for Savannah," Donland informed Jackson. "Have we enough fresh water and stores?"

"Aye, I set about filling the water casks. Mr. Aldridge is leading the party," Jackson answered then asked, "Something amiss?"

"Seems I'm the fleet's messenger boy, *Hornet* a packet vessel." He answered flatly.

"Aye, I thought as much, all for the good of the service! But answer me honest, would you rather be fourth on that hulk yonder or be the messenger boy for the fleet?"

Donland's face reddened. "Old son watch your tongue!" he snapped and instantly regretted. Jackson had put the peg in the hole.

"It is I who should hold my tongue. That was uncalled for," he apologized.

Jackson grinned, "Pardon my impertinence Sir! It'll not happen again."

They both laughed.

The café was crowed for the evening meal. Donland and Jackson sat across from one another relaxing after a meal of chicken, rice, stewed tomatoes and fried plantains. They were drinking the local wine which was at best better than water. Doctor Fredricks was at a table in a dark corner drinking and not eating. Donland was keeping an eye on the fellow. It was one thing to be drunk but quite another to make himself a nuance with the women of the café.

"What will you do with that fellow?" Jackson asked.

"Watch him until he passes out and then have him hauled back to *Hornet*."

"But he has no orders and can't be carried in the muster book."

"Aye, but he is a surgeon nonetheless and we may well have need of his services. No one in Antigua will protest his absence."

"Aye!"

"But sober, surely he will demand his rights."

Donland had considered this. "He may not be carried in our muster book for wages but we may carry him for victuals since we have orders to deliver him and carry him as a passenger. I shall of course not reveal that to him. Should the clerks in the admiralty inquire into his status that will between him and them. As I said, I can produce written orders as to him being a passenger."

Jackson was thoughtful and lifted his glass to drink. "Did you notice that once we took his liquor supply he did not complain?"

"Aye, that was a queer thing. I was also aware he only left his cabin to go to the head. Samson gave me a written report once a day. Basically, the man spent all his time reading the books he brought aboard and writing in a journal."

"Reading what?" Jackson asked.

"I put that to Samson, and he reported all the books were of a medical nature. I believe the man may prove to be a very competent surgeon."

One of the young girls serving food came too close to Fredricks, and he made a grab for her. She shrieked, but no one gave notice save Donland and Jackson. Fredricks had settled back into his chair, his chin on his chest. They returned to their wine, talk and cigars. Once the cigars and wine were finished, Donland stood to leave.

The wine or strong drink that Fredricks had been imbibing took its toll, and the man was passed out slumping in his chair.

"Shall I take him across?" Jackson asked.

"Aye," Donland answered. "We'll both go. It will take all we can summon to carry that much dead weight."

Donland moved to one side of Fredricks and Jackson to the other. The man was cold. What Donland thought was spilled wine on the man's front wasn't wine but blood. "Avast!" Donland said. "Put him down."

Jackson complied and Donland took a candle from a table and held it close to Fredricks. It was blood; blood from the slit in the man's neck.

"The girl," Jackson said.

"Aye, that would be my guess. Probably revenge for something he did either to her or one of her family."

"A neat job of it," Jackson said.

"Aye, that it is. I shall go report it to the flag lieutenant, the reports will be his to do. You best go to *Hornet*."

"Aye Sir," Jackson grinned. "He's not entered into our muster thank God!"

Coutts was not pleased with Donland's statement. "You say that a girl did it, one of the serving girls at the café? I find that rather difficult to believe."

"Those are the facts as I stated. No other person went near to the doctor."

"The facts as you state them. I can assure you that there will be an inquiry."

Donland did not like the direction Coutts was taking the conversation. "I would suggest then that you fetch the provost and accompany me to the café. Let us be done with this affair before I sail on the morning tide."

Coutts's face showed red. "That would be most irregular, and as to your sailing on the tide, that would be a matter for the provost."

It was Donland's turn to burn with anger. "When the tide makes in the morning *Hornet* will be on it. I have my orders! There are to be no delays!"

Their voices had reached enough volume for two marine guards to come down the stairs. A short plumb man wearing a lieutenant's coat followed. "What the blazes are you two shouting about?" the lieutenant asked.

"There's been a murder Mr. Newland, the surgeon Doctor Fredricks."

"By thunder why wasn't I called?"

"Coutts explained, "Mr. Donland only just arrived, and I was about to inform you."

The short man introduced himself, "Commander Donland I am Lieutenant Newland, the Provost."

Coutts explained, "he was killed in a café where Mr. Donland was dining and he tells me that a servant girl did it."

"Mmmph, yes, she may well have," Newland said. "More than one woman on this island has cause."

Newland turned his attention to Hinson, "Sergeant Hinson, roust out Lockaby and that useless Fitz-Simmons. Have them make arrangements for burial. You go along to the café and make inquires. Report to me in the morning."

"But Mr. Newland, the *Hornet* will be on the tide in the morning," Coutts protested.

Leland scowled, "And well he should be. I'm certain he had no part in this affair for he is of good and honorable reputation. Fredricks' loss will trouble no one."

As he was being rowed to *Hornet*, Donland considered Leland's words, "good and honorable reputation". It was comforting to know there were those on Antigua that had flattering words about him. After the treatment he received from Coutts and Admiral Rowley's Lassiter, it was indeed welcome to be spoken well of!

CHAPTER SIX

The larboard six-pounders fired one at a time like rolling thunder.

A man was down, blood pumped from his mangled leg. Two men ripped the shirts from their backs and attempted to staunch the blood. Andrews pulled one man back and kneeled beside the stricken man. He pulled a handkerchief from his pocket and jammed it into the wound. Quickly he pulled the man's belt from his waist then cinched it tight over the handkerchief. "Get him below to the orlop, I'll be down soon. Don't remove that belt!" Andrews commanded.

Donland saw and heard what was said and done.

"Load!" Andrews shouted to the idle gun crews.

Donland stood at the railing looking down at his watch as he timed the gun crews. The thunder rolled again.

"Secure the guns Mr. Andrews," Donland commanded.

This had been the second time the crews had fired their weapons since coming aboard. The mid-morning weather was about perfect for the hot work. The wind was good, the sea calm and a scattering of clouds kept the sun from broiling the men's brains and backs.

"Mr. Jackson exercise the starboard guns, practice only. Lord knows they shall need to be better in the coming days. Weather permitting, every day they are to have two hours of practice. I shall go below!" Donland stated.

Andrews was still at his station supervising the securing of the larboard guns. Donland said, "go below Mr. Andrews and see to your injured man."

"Aye Sir," Andrews answered and hurried from the deck.

Donland followed Andrews below. He was curious.

When Donland reached the orlop, he stopped at the bottom of the hatchway. Andrews had the injured man's trousers off. The belt was still cinched tight around the wound.

"Lars, fetch a two pints of rum from the purser," Andrews ordered. And then, "Miller get the strap."

Andrews removed his coat and was unbuttoning his shirt when he saw Donland. Their eyes met but neither said anything. The stricken man was wailing and doing his best to get at his injured leg but Bill, the former slave, was holding the man down by his shoulders.

Lars returned with the rum. "Pour it down his gullet!" Andrews ordered and Lars did so. The man gagged and spit but swallowed most of it.

Miller passed Andrews the leather strap and Miller ordered, "lift his head Miller." Miller did and Andrews quickly stuffed the middle of the strap into the man's mouth and tied the ends firmly behind the man's head securing the gag.

Donland saw the man's eyes grow wide with horror. They both knew what Andrews intended. "Artery is cut clean through; you'll be dead if I don't cut it off," Andrews said as in a comforting tone.

Samson clambered down the hatchway and sidestepped Donland. He was carrying a glowing red short iron bar with a thick wooden handle. Donland had seen one used before and knew the stench of burning flesh was to come.

Andrews knew his business and commanded, "get the saw Miller, Lars help hold him down."

Donland watched the gruesome surgery as the leg was sawed off. The man passed out. When the leg was off, Andrews let the leg drop to the deck and he took the hot iron from Samson. Donland heard the hissing and saw steam rising. The man did not even flinch.

"He's dead Sir," Lars said.

Andrews stopped with the iron and looked at the injured man's face. Then he bent to the man's mouth with his ear. He sighed and said, "get some canvas and sew him up."

Donland's eyes met Andrews. Andrews turned away, "Bill, get me some water to wash off with and clean up this lot."

"Aye!" Bill replied and dashed up the hatchway past Donland.

Donland stood. Overhead he heard the rumble of the starboard guns as the men rolled them out and then rolled them back simulating loading and firing. It was then he remembered the dead man's name, Heartwell from Essex, a good topman. His skill would be missed.

A knock at the door signaled Andrews' presence. "Come!" Donland called to him.

Andrews entered with his hat under his arm.

"Sit there Mr. Andrews," Donland commanded.

Andrews obeyed and Donland said, "Samson bring the bottle."

"It's brandy," he said to Andrews without bothering to ask if Andrews wanted the wine.

Samson brought two glasses and a half full bottle then served Andrews. He sat the bottle down on Donland's desk.

"I thought you would need that after what you just did," Donland said.

"Aye Sir," Andrews said but did not drink.

Donland waited and when Andrews did not drink he said, "drink it down and pour another. It'll steady your nerves."

Andrews obeyed.

"Had you sawed a man's leg off before?" Donland asked.

Andrews set the bottle down and replied with a note of solemnest in his voice, "no Sir."

They sat without speaking for a long minute, neither drinking. Then Andrews filled his glass again and drank the contents.

"My father is a doctor," Andrews stated and then continued, "I had occasion to assist him."

"And you chose the sea instead of medicine?" Donland asked.

"Aye!" Andrews answered.

"Let us pray that your skills will not be put to the test again," Donland said.

Andrews' face clouded then tinged with red. "I did what I could, but the artery was torn length wise; he lost too much blood. Poor bugger didn't have a chance!"

Donland did not let his voice betray his emotion. He had known when he had observed the spurting blood that Heartwell was doomed. Even a skilled surgeon could not have saved the man but Andrews had tried. Not only that but he had cared and Donland had seen that as well.

"Men die Mr. Andrews, some because they are careless or because others are careless. We may punish the living for their mistakes but there is ought we can do to the dead. We can also reward the living but it is pointless to do some for the dead. I was pleased that you did two things, first you assessed the injured man and second you continued with your duty after he was carried below. Have you been in battle before?"

Andrews' face showed confusion.

"I take it you have not," Donland said then went on, "in battle men are injured and die; men under your charge, men of your division. You will see them fall and for a moment your heart will ache but your duty must come first. Should you allow an attachment to cloud your judgment or your response, others will die.

Andrews sighed heavily, "aye Sir."

Donland smiled. The three glasses of brandy had the effect upon Andrews he had hoped for. Andrews' eyes were bright and his speech a little delayed.

"I believe it is Mr. Dewitt's watch, and yours is to follow. Go to your hammock and sleep off the brandy Mr. Andrews, I'll not have an officer standing watch that can't stand."

As Andrews exited Welles was at the door. "Mr. Dewitt's compliments sir, Anguilla is sighted."

"Thank you Mr. Welles, I shall go up."

"Mr. Jackson two more men in the trees, we need more eyes aloft."

"Aye Sir," Jackson answered.

"Mr. Dewitt we will tack to the east."

"Aye Sir."

"We'll run northeast until the island is out of sight."

Dewitt had advised him at the start of the mission to avoid being seen by the Spanish at Anguilla as they have a small garrison and a Spanish squadron was known to be patrolling the Leeward Islands' passages. The more sea between them and the island the safer they will be. *Hornet* was no match for a frigate even a Spanish one. The six-pounders couldn't match the nines of a frigate.

The sails were still coming round when a man shouted down, "Sail to nor'west!"

Donland pulled a glass from the rack and grasped the shrouds. He swung round and began climbing.

"Two sail!" The lookout called."

Donland reached the crosstrees and put the glass to his eye. He found the closer ship and adjusted the view. She was two-masted and square-sailed close-hauled toward *Hornet*. He checked his own sails and was relieved to see the tack was completed. In a matter of minutes he would know the stranger's intentions.

As he watched the ship grew larger. There was no doubt, she was a frigate, Spanish! Suddenly her sails started to go round. She tacked to intercept him. There was no hope of sailing past on this course without coming in range of her guns. He made his decision. He shouted down, "Mr. Dewitt call all hands! Wear ship!"

"Aye Sir!" Dewitt called up.

Dawkins, the bosom mate, was cursing and calling hands. Jackson's booming voice was shouting orders. Donland watched the oncoming ship. She completed her tack and *Hornet*'s Sails began to move. "Belay wearing!" he shouted. "Braces there haul back!"

He continued watching the oncoming ship and was relieved that their sails were coming round as they sought to match *Hornet*'s in order to intercept. The captain of the oncoming ship had watched intently and anticipated giving the order when he saw *Hornet* begin to wear ship. The captain's haste was his undoing.

"T'gallents!" Donland called down.

Donland watched as Bill and the former slaves swarmed the rigging and in what he considered masterful seamanship, release the bundled sails. He turned and without the glass saw clearly that the approaching frigate was in the process of coming back to her previous course. She would be too late to intercept but not too late to run out are guns and bring *Hornet* within range. He raced back down the rigging to the deck.

To the west the smaller sail that had been trailing the frigate set her course toward Puerto Rico. Donland judged her to be a costal trader and wanted no part of what was coming. The frigate would be more than enough to deal with.

Their best bet would be to out distance her if they could get by her without taking a beating.

"Helm! Two points to port!" Donland called. The more sea room he could gain from the frigate the better. Still her guns will be able to hit even at that range. They were closing fast; no more than a league separated them. He expected to see her gun ports open any second. He studied her, she was closed hauled and without tacking could not close the gap abeam.

Donland was aware that every man aboard *Hornet* was holding their breath. They knew as he did that the metal the Don could hurl would do grave damage. If a mast were hit, they would be doomed. The frigate could then tack and take them at her leisure. The distance separating them was growing, but they were not out of long-cannon shot range. Still, the Don waited, waited too long by Donland's estimation. He was about to heave a sigh of relief when a lookout called down.

"Two sail off the port quarter!"

Donland pulled himself upon the shrouds and put the glass to his eye. "That's why he didn't fire!" he said to himself as he saw two sloops coming after *Hornet* with every stitch of sail they had hoisted. The frigate had meant to delay and hem him in toward the island. The sloops would have been stationed to catch sight of the topsails of ships near the island. It was a plan that had evidently worked well for the Spanish.

Donland shouted to Dewitt, "Mr. Dewitt we are being chased. Put every rag we have on the sticks. Make her fly! Beat to quarters!"

The sloops could not catch them but that wasn't their intent. The odds of clearing Scrub Island were few. Even as he considered this he saw the frigate wearing ship to go about. The two dogs would chase but the frigate would run abeam keeping the distance no more than a long cannon shot. The island with its deadly reefs was the stopper in the bottle.

He looked up, the sails were straining, to the east there was the hint of a squall but too far to aid him. Speed would be their only salvation providing they could weather the island. He had no more than three leagues to gain safety.

"Fine fair day," Jackson stated.

"Aye," Donland answered. "The trap is sprung, they intend to pin us to the island."

"Aye, that they will do," Jackson said casually. "The dogs will stay at our heels. They've played this game before."

"Are you suggesting that they are confident of their quarry?"

"Aye, they are and should be," Jackson answered and pointed at the frigate. "See that bow wave, she's cutting the water without a care in the world."

Donland studied her for a moment. He looked back at the two sloops. "Mr. Jackson throw some full barrels over the stern not empty ones mind you. We shall make them think we are lightening the ship."

Jackson looked questioning at Donland and was about to ask, "Why?" but did not.

Donland nodded and grinned, The reason you will know shortly. While the barrels are going over get a sea anchor ready. I shall have a word with Mr. Dewitt."

Jackson still looked confused but reluctantly said, "aye Sir."

"Remember Jackson the stern, everything goes over the stern!"

Dewitt was amazed at the daring of the idea but answered. "aye Sir."

Jackson and his selected men were throwing barrels over the stern. Donland noticed three men were busy with the sea anchor. "Is it ready?" he asked.

Lars replied, "aye Sir."

"Ball it up, make it small and put it over the stern," Donland ordered.

They obeyed and almost instantly the effect was felt. The sails remained full but their speed was reduced by more than a knot.

"Stand by with an axe Lars. When I give the order cut those lines and set it loose."

"Aye Sir," Lars answered looking just as confused as Jackson had earlier.

Donland stood for ten long seconds watching the frigate. He was delighted to see her pulling away from them ever so slowly. He prayed it was enough. Turning, he estimated the sloops were shortening the distance quickly. He doubted they carried anything more than six-pounders. With the sea anchor dragging behind them they had little more than thirty minutes before the sloops would fire ranging shots. He would wait as long as he dared. Everything depended on the frigate not noticing that they were out-pacing their quarry. It was a gamble, but it was the only option.

"She fired!" the lookout called down.

Donland turned but did not see the splash of shot. The Don had fired too soon. He took out his watch. He would give it five minutes more.

"Mr. Jackson two more barrels!" he shouted. He had to make the Dons think he was still running.

The minutes dragged by and the sloops were closing, they would fire again soon. The good side of things was that the frigate was still out-distancing *Hornet.* There was going to be room. He decided to wait no longer.

"Now Lars! Cut those lines!" Donland commanded.

"Wear ship!" Dewitt shouted!" The men were already stationed, ready for the order.

Donland watched with delight as the sails went round. The men worked like mad men, they may not have understood why but they sensed their lives were at stake. Sail and rudder shot the *Hornet* forward to cross the wake of the frigate. The sloops were no longer of any consequence, only sea room away from the frigate mattered. She could tack and give chase but she was a knot or more slower now. *Hornet*'s only danger would be a crippling shot. He was gambling the starboard side guns were not manned and loaded.

The sloops had changed course to give chase. Again Donland was gambling on *Hornet*'s speed and the sloop's commanders not willing to make a long sea chase.

They crossed the frigate's wake as she was wearing ship. They were slow; his maneuver had caught them off guard. Their confidence in their trap was their folly. They cleared her wake and were still near enough to see faces. "Too close!" Donland said to himself. The name on the stern read *Vengador* which meant *Avenger* in English.

Three chains abeam of the frigate a gun port opened. Five chains more two more ports were open. *Hornet* surged on keeling with the wind full abeam, Dewitt was calling adjustment to the sails, at a quarter of a league the frigate was turning; she fired. The ball was poorly aimed and fell well short of *Hornet*'s stern. Two more shots followed sending spray over *Hornet*'s quarter. The next shot was from almost half a league away and fell a chain's length in front of *Hornet*. Donland's gut was tight waiting for the next ball that would surely hit *Hornet*. To his surprise and to his joy the next shot fell short as did the next. He turned and saw that the sloops had given up the chase. The men began to cheer. Huzza! Huzza! Huzza!

"Keep the wind at our backs Mr. Dewitt!" Donland called.

Then to Jackson he called, "Mr. Jackson you have the deck. Once we are well clear, give the men a tot of rum. Our people have done well this day!"

"Aye Sir, that they have and their commander as well."

Donland went below. His clothes were sodden with sweat and his heart was still pounding. The trap had been neatly set and executed. Were it not for the Don's over confidence *Hornet* would be a prize. He had learned a valuable lesson which was never to assume that events will play out as anticipated. Over confidence could wreck a ship as easily as a broadside. No, it would be better to give enemies the benefit of their cunning.

Sailors were busy restoring the bulkheads and carrying the captain's possessions back to his cabin. He stood waiting to be alone. Samson came in unbidden carrying a tray with a bottle and a glass. The bottle was unfamiliar. "What have you Samson?" Donland asked.

Samson smiled and set the tray on the desk. He lifted the bottle and poured a clear liquid into the glass, no more than a finger. Samson then offered the glass. Donland took it and sniffed. There was no odor. He put it to his lips, rolled it around his tongue and found it all but tasteless. He swallowed, it went down smoothly and then the fire hit. He sucked air and involuntarily shook his whole body.

When he could speak he stuttered, "What, what is that Devil's brimstone?"

Samson took a stub of a pencil from his pocket and wrote on the desk, slave liquor and under that potato. He then lifted the bottle to pour again.

"No, one is enough!" Donland managed. "Rum or wine Samson; no more of that."

A knock at the door claimed his attention.

"Mr. Dewitt's compliments Sir. He requests you come on deck."

"Problem Mr. Welles?" Donland inquired.

The boy's face flushed, and he said, "no Sir, not that he stated."

"We've too much sail for this heading," Dewitt stated.

Donland looked up. Dewitt was right.

"Mr. Dewitt I trust your judgment. I know that many captains deem it necessary to be called before reducing sail or making any alterations but I'm not one of them. On your watch *Hornet* is completely in your hands."

Dewitt did not answer or show any emotion, he merely nodded slightly. Then he asked, "course Sir?"

Donland considered the question; he had been considering it before going below. Turning back to their original course might well be what the frigate's captain would guess. If he did, he would have bent on all the sail he could muster in hopes of intercepting *Hornet.* "Due north Mr. Dewitt, due north. We shall stay well out in deep water before turning west."

"Aye Sir," Dewitt answered.

Donland stayed on deck through the next watch. The men went about their tasks with good humor and efficiency. He was a bit amazed at how well they had adapted to each other and to *Hornet.* Of the ships he had served in, this ship's company appeared to him on the surface to be as good if not better than the others. Perhaps that he was so far removed from them as captain that he was not privy to the pettiness that existed. Nor was there any slackness of duty apparent whenever he was on deck. He well remembered how that as a midshipman and lieutenant that when the captain would come on deck every jack and every officer stood a little taller, talked less and did their best not to draw the captain's attention. But then again, *Hornet*'s punishment book contained very few entries. Either Jackson and Andrews were doing a suburb job of handling the men or he wasn't being told of infractions. He would have to inquire of Jackson.

He remembered how it had been when he commanded the prize Morgador; the men had come to Jackson with their day-to-day grievances. It had been Jackson who had dealt with the routine punishments. It should not surprise him that these same men would follow the pattern that they were familiar with. It was certainly less formal than what took place on any ship in which he had previously served. Perhaps he was too lax on these men? He did not know, but as he paced it occurred to him that if the men were happy as things were and the ship was efficient in all respects, then he should be pleased. As someone once said, a happy ship's company is a dependable ship's company and reflects well upon her captain. Yes, he should be more than pleased.

He was also more than pleased with Dewitt. The man knew how to get the best out of *Hornet.* What had surprised him most and pleased him most about the man was that he showed no animosity toward the black crewmen. As an American, most regarded slaves as less than human and were to be treated as such. Dewitt seemed to take a Quaker attitude towards the former slaves. To him they were just men, men who worked as he worked, men who served the captain as he served the captain. It was his lot in life as it was theirs. There again the notion stuck him to ask Jackson, he would know the man by now.

A knock at the door heralded David's arrival.

"Pardon Sir, my watch has ended, and I wanted to ask a question," David stated.

Donland smiled. It is unheard of for a midshipman to knock at his captain's door to ask a question. But, David wasn't yet aware of the lofty distance between captain and midshipman. And, the boy had a special place in his heart.

"Ask?"

"How did you know the frigate would outpace us and not slow when we slowed with the sea anchor?"

Again Donland smiled. "A very wise captain said, 'Use what your enemy gives you against him. It matters not if it is wind, a lee shore, or even his own confidence, use it against him.' I remembered those words as I took note of how confident the frigate's captain was. His trap had worked before and he was confident we would be snared. Were he more vigilant we would have been his victim."

David's eyes were wide with understanding. "I shall remember Sir."

"See that you do," he said then stood. "Now repeat what the wise captain told me."

David did not hesitate and answered, "use what your enemy gives you against him."

"That's correct and remember your enemy may not give you much. Victory or defeat lies in the small details that are often overlooked. It has been stated this way; for want of a nail the shoe was lost. For want of a shoe the horse was lost. For want of a horse the rider was lost. For want of a rider the battle was lost. For want of a battle the kingdom was lost. And all for the want of a horseshoe nail. Do you understand?"

"Aye Sir."

"Here, I shall write it down and when next we talk, you will repeat for me."

David smiled, "aye Sir that I will."

As he handed the scrap of paper over he asked, "Do you have another question?

"Aye, will we have a battle?"

"Mmm, I would hazard that this is the question plaguing the wardroom mess. It was always the question when I was a midshipman." He paused then continued, "the sailor's lot is always the unknown. Whether it be a storm or cannon we don't know what is over the horizon. What we do know is the uncertainty of how we will face our fear at the time of testing. Brave talk among our messmates bolsters our own resolve but can't be counted on when those same fellows lie bleeding and mangled on the deck. No, what is inside a man has to be strength of character not words. When your messmates flounder or fall, you must stand-to and lead not because of brave words but because it is who you are.

Will there be a battle, not if we are vigilant, for our orders are to be swift as birds and as canny as foxes."

"Sir?" Confusion was in the boy's voice.

Donland laughed, "I confuse myself sometimes. But what I mean is that our orders are to sail as fast as possible carrying dispatches for the fleet. We are to avoid entanglements with the enemy if at all possible because the dispatches we carry will determine when and if there is a great sea fight. It is not glorious, but it is of the highest importance."

"Aye Sir."

"Now back to your mess," Donland ordered.

CHAPTER SEVEN

By dawn *Hornet* had logged a hundred and twenty miles or so from the Don's trap. The rhyme red sky at morning, shepherd take warning ran through Donland's head. It wasn't hurricane season but fierce gales were not unknown in these latitudes. Most crept in from the west and died but occasionally a strong one with cold currents would sweep down with ferocity to rip the sticks right out of a vessel.

Donland stood in the bow with a glass scanning the horizon for a line of cloud.

"Rouge wind Captain?" Jackson asked.

"Aye, has the feel for it does it not?"

"Mr. Dewitt agrees, coming straight down from Florida then sucking everything up toward New York."

Donland rubbed his chin and looked up at the sky. He thought the wind a bit cool on his cheek. "Have Mr. Dewitt shorten sail and we shall lie to. We shall prepare all the hatches and ports for a gale. Double the lashings on the sails."

"Aye Sir, better to be prudent," Jackson answered.

"Walk with me Mr. Jackson while we have a moment," Donland said.

"Aye Sir," Jackson answered as he fell into step with Donland.

"What of Dewitt?" Donland asked in a hushed voice.

Jackson did not hesitate, "A capable seaman in all respects."

Donland nodded and continued walking. The subject was broached.

They walked on until reaching the bowsprit and Donland stopped. A half-dozen men were at work repairing and splicing lines and rigging on either side of the bowsprit. They ignored the presence of their betters but none spoke.

Jackson said to them, "You men lay aft until I call for you."

There was no surprise in the men's faces. They laid aside their tools, rose and wordlessly started aft.

When no one was within earshot Jackson asked, "You want to know about the man not his abilities?"

"Aye," Donland answered.

"The bones of the man he has told you. He's been knocked about by nobs and toffs so he isn't beholding to any. Never married," Jackson paused thoughtfully. "Somewhat like you, not a drinker nor a gambling man, bit pious by jack-tar standards. By my estimation I'd say the man takes it as it comes and gives no quarter."

Donland took a deep breath and held it turning his attention to the far horizon. He phrased the question in his mind before asking, "Can he be trusted?"

Without hesitation Jackson answered, "Aye!"

Satisfied Donland said, "Call your men back to their duties. You are a fair man and read the weather gauge better than most."

Donland, Jackson and Dewitt were on deck watching the clouds roiling and rolling as they approached *Hornet.*

"It'll hit hard and be done in half-an-hour!" Dewitt stated. "Seen em' come like this before."

Donland tried not to show fascination. He felt like a kid as he watched the oncoming clouds. He well remembered the hurricane that had ripped men from trees when they had beached Morgador for repairs. Those howling winds made breathing difficult and speech impossible. He wondered how the wind of this storm would compare. He remembered his father saying when a thunderstorm had sweep across the valley where they lived, "Behold the very breath of Almighty God!" The hurricane hadn't seemed like the breath of God, it bore more resemblance to the wrath of God.

They felt the storm before it arrived. A fresh wind tinged with cold. In these tropical latitudes any hint of cold was as out of place as a virgin in a whorehouse. But yet, here it was and then suddenly there was a rush of wind bow on and *Hornet* rose up and her bow came round. She began to keel larboard and there was nothing that could be done. She bucked and came down hard with water spaying over her railing. In an instant she rose up again and the rain, hard and cold began to beat down.

Donland was aware of screaming from behind him. He turned to see one helmsman was down; his face spewing blood so fast the rain couldn't wash it away. The man writhed in agony. The second helmsman was hanging on for dear life as the wheel spun one way and then the other. Jackson was already moving toward the wheel.

Something overhead carried away and thudded onto the deck at Donland's feet. Just as he looked up a line whipped across his jaw stinging him and drawing blood. Before he could draw his handkerchief, Samson was there pressing something against the wound. He pushed Samson away, "You men! He called to two men huddled beside the binnacle, "tidy that rabble and make fast!"

Donland looked on as Jackson pushed the injured man away from the helm. Dewitt dropped to his knees and pressed a hand over the wound to stem the flow of blood.

"Hold her Jackson!" Donland shouted.

Then to the men on the yards, "Get sail off her!"

Another burst of strong wind hit *Hornet* and the jib sail blew apart.

"Make secure there!" Donland shouted.

The cold came on them as suddenly as stepping out of a warm cozy inn into a New England nor' easterner. Donland felt it and shivered.

The calm and the sudden drop of temperature came upon *Hornet* as her way came off her. No man aboard said a word above a whisper. It was an eerie silence, a harbinger of death itself.

"Wave coming!" Dewitt shouted.

Every man aboard *Hornet* was instantly alert, eyes searching for the wave.

Jackson's shout broke the tension, "You there! Another set of hands on the wheel!"

The seaman, Gaston by name, short and stocky with powerful arms came from out of his trance and made for the wheel.

"Dead Sir!" Dewitt said as he stood beside Donland. For a moment Donland didn't understand, then he did, the man on the deck had died from the blow to his head.

The wave that struck *Hornet* before Donland could speak came bow on and lifted the ship as it were just a large gentle swell.

"That's the worst of it," Dewitt said. "Damnable cold!" he added

"Aye," Donland answered. "Make sail Mr. Dewitt."

"Mr. Jackson, call the watch!" he added in the next breath.

"Mr. Jackson's compliments Sir, Tybee light in sight," Aldridge reported.

"Very well, I shall come on deck. Make our number and be prepared for the recognition signal," Donald said as he slid the sealed packet into his coat.

"Aye Sir," Aldridge replied and hurried from the cabin.

Donland studied the lighthouse and the approach to Tybee Island. There was a small battery a chain's distance from the lighthouse. He was sure there would be other batteries; he would take note of each one. This would be his first time in Savannah and doubted it would be his last and if those batteries ever changed hands, he would need to know their locations.

Overhead the mail pendant was flying. Those in the lighthouse would certainly see the pendant and send word by horseback to the governor's house of his approach. If all was as it should be they would enter the roads and wait to be acknowledged. He would not venture further toward the city until he was sure it was in British hands and not the colonials.

The men were at quarters. He had decided to take no chances. Savannah would not be the first city to have changed hands since the colonials had raised armies and militias. Captain Yorke's orders were clear on the matter of not anchoring at Savannah until it was established that the city was under British control.

Dewitt was handling the ship as they approached the inlet to enter into the roads. He had been in and out of Savannah on many occasions and assured Donland that he would be able to get them in and then out in a hurry if necessary. "There are more than a few banks and the currents change with the seasons. We will do well to keep all the water we can find under the keel and should we need to run, the more room and water the better."

Donland agreed with Dewitt's assessment. There were two men in the chains casting lead. Running onto a mud bank while under fire would be disastrous.

"By the mark four," the leadsman cried out.

"Quarter less four," another voice sang out.

"By the mark four," came the first voice.

"By the mark four," the second voice now called.

"Guard boat coming off!" a lookout called down.

"We'll know soon," Jackson said as he and Donland located the guard boat.

Donland glanced up; the four marines were in the tops.

"Heave to Mr. Dewitt," Donland ordered.

"Aye Sir," Dewitt replied.

"Mr. Jackson prepare to receive our visitors. I see only a midshipman. I'll go below."

"Aye Sir."

The midshipman that came aboard was from the fifty-gun frigate Experiment under the command of Captain Wallace, the senior naval officer on station. The midshipman was a chubby boy of about sixteen with a ruddy red complexion to go with his red hair.

"Captain Wallace's compliments Sir, you are to report to him forthwith."

The boy's tone was snobbish and that set Donland's temperament accordingly. "Is Captain Wallace senior on this station?" Donland asked.

"Aye," the boy replied leaving off the "Sir".

Donland ignored the surly tone and lack of respect. "Is Vice-Admiral Arbuthnot in Savannah?"

"He is not but Captain Wallace commands here."

The boy's tone was becoming intolerable. "What is your name?"

"Augustus Stuart, heir to the Earl of Bute!"

Donland showed no recognition and said, “my compliments to Captain Wallace and I shall come aboard within the hour.”

The round face turned beet red and before the boy could speak Donland added, “a midshipman is to address the captain of His Majesty's vessels as Sir. Return to your ship and when I come aboard, I would not care to see your face. Is that understood?”

Stuart's face twisted, and he snarled, “it is by God!”

Donland jumped to his feet his anger building, “your insolence will not be tolerated. You will not return to your ship until you show proper respect!”

Stuart hand moved to his dirk and with sudden speed Samson was behind him and he placed his massive hand on the boy's arm. The boy tried to twist away but was held firm. He saw into Samson's eyes and stopped struggling.

“I'll have you flogged!” Stuart boasted.

Samson tightened his grip on the boy's forearm. Stuart grimaced in pain.

“Mr. Stuart,” Donland said sternly, “when proper respect is shown you may leave and not until then!”

The fight was gone out of the boy, however, his face still held malice. Samson placed his other hand on the boy's shoulder and swiftly turned the boy to face him.

Donland could not see Stuart's face but he could see Samson's, it was a face of controlled rage.

Samson then spun the boy around to face Donland.

Donland wanted to laugh; the boy was white with fear.

“Are you ready to depart Mr. Stuart?” Donland asked.

Stuart hesitated then said meekly, “Aye Sir.”

“Very well, report to Captain Wallace.”

Captain Wallace held to naval discipline and regulations having turned out the side party for Donland's arrival. He was greeted with all the pomp due a post captain. Marines slapped their muskets as they presented arms. And keeping with tradition and naval discipline, Donland saluted the flag and doffed his hat to the quarterdeck.

Wallace came forward and extended his hand and then began introducing his officers. Donland noted the absence of Stuart. Whether it was the young noble's choice or Captain Wallace had gotten wind of the boy's disrespect, he didn't know. He assumed the latter as sailors have good ears when it came to hearing conversations in the captain's quarters.

Donland noted that the Wallace's cabin on the frigate was spacious compared with his own cabin in the *Hornet.* He also noted the thick rug that covered most of the deck space. Most captains merely have the deck painted in some pattern they favor. It was evident to him that Wallace was either well to do or had been fortunate in prize money.

A black servant entered the cabin carrying a silver tray with two glasses and a cut-glass decanter and held two smaller trays with assorted cheeses and meats.

"Have a seat Captain Donland," Wallace invited and indicated a red leather covered stylish chair.

"Refreshment?" Wallace asked.

"Thank you Sir," Donland replied and accepted a glass and selected a bite of cheese while the servant poured wine.

Wallace also took a glass but not cheese or meat.

He took a sip from the glass. Wallace got to the point, "What are your orders Captain Donland?"

Donland carefully placed his glass on the deck beside the chair and drew the oilskin packet from his coat and withdrew a letter. "I'm to pass this to the senior on station here if Vice-Admiral Arbuthnot is not present. My orders are to report to him with dispatches as swiftly as possible."

Wallace took the letter and read the contents. "So the Spaniards and the French both will be on the hunt for us," he said flatly.

"Aye Sir."

"And what of *Hornet*, any encounters with our enemies?

"Aye Sir," Donland answered and reached into another pocket of his coat and came out with his written report."

Wallace again read, taking more time than he had with the first letter. No doubt he would digest its contents more fully when alone. He looked up and grinned at Donland, "You must have been very crafty to escape LeFoaud's trap. He has snared a number of ships off that coast with his frigate and sloops. I suspect his main mission is to intercept our communications."

"Aye Sir."

"Will you join me for dinner tonight?" Wallace asked.

"Thank you Sir but I should be off with the evening tide for Vice-Admiral Arbuthnot."

"I understand. You will find him off the coast of Charles Town but before you go, I would like to send along a passenger who also has information to pass to the admiral."

"Will you also have dispatches?" Donland asked.

"Aye, I shall send them along with your passenger."

The passenger was James Boyd an Irishman full of bluster and dressed in a colonel's uniform. With him were three men, one of which was a servant. The other two wore captain uniforms.

"We shall go ashore at Winyah Bay it's up the coast from Charles Town," Boyd explained. "If you make your rendezvous with your ships first, then take us on afterwards."

Donland wanted to object but Captain's Wallace's orders were that *Hornet* would deliver Boyd and his companions along the Carolina coast as Boyd directed. The complication would come if they intercepted the Vice-Admiral's squadron first. The admiral may make other arrangements or have new orders. He was feeling more like a packet captain than a naval officer.

Four days later after continual tacking against as cold a wind as he could remember they were off Charles Town. There was no sign of the admiral's squadron. One tack brought *Hornet* close enough to Sullivan's Island for the battery to try a ranging shot. They sailed on into contrary winds and one gale after another. Five bells in the afternoon they sighted Cape San Roman. They put the launch over the side in the midst of a gale with four marines eight crewman and Boyd's party. Lieutenant Andrews was in command of the launch.

"Put them ashore but don't you go ashore," Donland commanded Andrews.

"Aye Sir," Andrews answered.

Donland watched as Boyd's party was landed and Andrews pushed off. They were fighting a strong current and high waves. The launch was having difficulty and more than once they faltered. Through the glass he watched Andrews yelling and waving his arms. They came through and were within hailing distance when the lookout hailed the deck.

"Sail to starboard!"

Donland spun in the direction. He couldn't see anything. The gale was blowing at three to four knots with heavy downpours every few minutes.

"Mr. Jackson prepare to get underway. As soon as we recover the launch, we'll stand out to sea."

"Mr. Dewitt two men on the helm if you please."

"Three sail!" The lookout called down to the deck.

"Where away?" Donland commanded.

"Starboard Sir!"

Donland pulled the most powerful telescope they had from the rack. There was too much weather to see the ships clear enough to make out whether they were friend or foe, merchant or men of war. Each had three masts and was as large as a fourth rate. *Hornet* was moving but making little headway. The oncoming ships would be on them before they could gain sea room. There was little choice.

"Mr. Jackson bring us about!" he commanded.

"Hands to the braces! Tacks and sheets!" Jackson bellowed.

With the helm hard over and the hands drawing the headsail sheets *Hornet* came round into the wind.

"Deck there!" The lookout called down. "Transports and a fifth rate!"

"Flag?" Donland shouted.

"Europa Sir!"

"The vice-admiral," Jackson stated.

"Aye!" Donland answered. "We'll lie-to until they catch up. Have the launch readied."

"Mr. Aldridge bend on, "have dispatches.'"

"Aye Sir," Aldridge answered as he hurried to find the correct flags for the message.

Donland was somewhat surprised upon meeting Vice-Admiral Arbuthnot. He had expected, after being piped aboard the Europa to hand off his packets to the flag captain. Instead he was met by flag lieutenant McPherson and escorted below to McPherson's small cabin to wait.

"I'll take the dispatches in to the admiral. His servant will bring some refreshment while you wait," McPherson said.

Donland handed over the packets and as McPherson was leaving the servant appeared with a tray bearing claret with assorted cheeses. The wine and the stability of the larger ship made him drowsy, so much so that he jumped up from the chair thinking he had fallen asleep. Checking his watch he realized he had been onboard almost an hour. He feared he had dozed off and been discovered my McPherson. If that were true surely McPherson would have been kind enough to wake him. He decided not to sit, better to stand that risk dozing. McPherson returned a few minutes later to fetch him.

Vice-Admiral Arbuthnot was an old man, seventy by the look at him. Too old to be at sea in Donland's thinking but he did appear to be hail and hearty. His hands did not shake, and he had all his teeth as far as Donland could see.

"Be seated commander," Arbuthnot commanded.

Donland sat.

"I've gone over all the dispatches and will be sending you back to Antigua when I have completed dispatches for Admiral Hyde-Parker," Arbuthnot said and went back to reading. It was some time before he laid aside a report and looking up saw Donland. He clearly had a puzzled expression.

"Yes, yes," Arbuthnot said more to himself than Donland.

"Commander, er Donland, I see that you command a local sloop, ah er, *Hornet.* Bit odd to send a vessel of that size to do packet duty. I would think she would be better served on the West Indies Station," Arbuthnot said and turned his attention to another report.

"Savannah, ah, Experiment, Captain Wallace." Arbuthnot said absent mindedly.

"Mr. Donland what of Savannah?"

He had not expected this question but knew he could not hesitate. "I have a good master and he brought us up the roads pass the Tybee light where we met the Experiment. I exchanged dispatches with her received Mr. Boyd and his party as passengers. Of Savannah, I saw no more than I could from the deck of *Hornet.*"

"Hmmpph. And what of Charles Town?"

This time he was ready. "We tacked in close enough that the colonials fired a ranging shot from Sullivan's Island. There was not much to observe."

Arbuthnot did not look up from the report he was holding and said, "Report back to your ship. Sail abreast of the last transport and keep station until we reach Savannah. I will have Lieutenant McPherson bring you orders and dispatches."

"Aye Sir," Donland answered as he stood.

The weather cleared as they reached Savannah. The flagship signaled for *Hornet* to stay off Tybee Island during the night. She was to prevent any unfamiliar craft from approaching the roads and the transports anchored inside. It was a fitful night of cold and wind as they tacked back and forth. Donland doubled the lookouts, and he remained on deck most of the night. Samson brought hot coffee on three occasions and each was scalding hot. Lieutenant McPherson came alongside midmorning.

"Admiral Arbuthnot's dispatches and your orders," he said curtly as he presented them to Donland.

"Something amiss?" Donland asked.

"I tell you Donland only that you may be aware of your blunder. The admiral was not pleased to hear of Doctor Fredrick's death. He faults you."

"Fault! I dare say there was no way I could have prevented his death. The man had been kept under watch the whole time I had charge of him. Even the moment of his death I was no more than twenty feet away as was my first lieutenant. Fault, no, heaven's no! If there is fault it was the man's own for abusing those women."

McPherson's face reddened, "yours was to prevent such an action, and you failed. The whole purpose of sending him aboard your ship was for his safety."

Donland cut him off, "Sir I was to deliver him to Hyde-Parker, but they refused him. He was a passenger, and I discharged him."

"You do not know then?"

"Know what?"

"He was the admiral's brother-in-law."

The statement was akin to a punch in the belly.

McPherson softened, "I best be off and you best sail as soon as I'm off. The admiral's gout is fitful and so is his mood."

CHAPTER EIGHT

"Mr. Jackson call all hands to make sail."

"Mr. Dewitt we shall go about to warmer climates. South by southeast!"

"Mr. Andrews come below to my cabin."

Hornet came around as Donland seated himself at his desk. Before him were the charts of the West Indies. His orders were to return to English Harbor with all haste and deliver dispatches and proceed to Hyde-Parker's squadron. "No delays, not for water nor stores!" his orders read.

A knock at the door heralded Andrews' arrival.

"Enter," Donland called.

Puzzlement was on Andrews' face.

Donland got right to the heart of his concerns. "Lieutenant Andrews did you know that Doctor Fredricks was brother-in-law to Vice Admiral Arbuthnot?"

Puzzlement was replaced by confusion. Andrews blinked and replied, "no Sir I did not."

Hornet heeled sharply and Donland and Andrews both reached for chairs to steady themselves. "Any hint at all that Fredricks is tied to peerage?"

"No Sir, the gossip was mostly confined to his activities and his drinking. I would venture no one on Antigua would have known. Certainly not from the man for he talked not at all of his life."

Donland sat.

Andrews stood with his hat under his arm looking confused. Donland considered telling Andrews of the conversation with McPherson but thought better of it. The less Andrews knew the better for them both.

Andrews asked, "Sir may I ask why Fredricks is important?"

Donland sighed, "at this juncture, no, the matter is of no consequence to you nor reflects upon your duty. Return to your station Mr. Andrews."

The puzzled look returned but Andrews managed, "aye Sir." He departed with his hat still under his arm.

Five bells in the forenoon Dewitt sent word to Donland, "Anguilla in sight."

Donland came on deck. There were a few clumps of cloud to the east and the wind was brisk from aft.

Seeing Donland, Dewitt announced, "all sail set."

"Very good Mr. Dewitt, we shall endeavor to pass without that Don's attention."

They logged another two hours of sailing and then the lookout called down, "Sail to starboard two points."

Donland heard the cry and hurried to the deck. Jackson was already climbing the shrouds to get a better look, so he decided to wait for his report.

"Sloop flying our colors."

Minutes dragged by like hours before Jackson spoke again. "Foremast staysail and mizzen staysail! Mainmast is bare, could be damaged!"

"Mr. Aldridge make our number."

Donland waited for the flags to be sent up.

"Alter course for her?" Dewitt asked.

Donland didn't hesitate, "No, we will hold our course."

"Recognition?" Donland called to Jackson

"No!" Jackson shouted down.

Donland frowned. "Mr. Dewitt do you think you would recognize her?"

"Aye if she's been in these waters."

"Very well, relieve Mr. Jackson."

Donland's attention was on Dewitt climbing and Jackson descending. He did not notice Bill approach.

"Beg pardon Sir."

Donland faced the man.

"I know her, she was Narciso but now I not know her name."

"How is it you know her Bill?" Donland asked.

"Blackbird, Espinoza owner. He on ship when you got us. Learned sailing on her first."

"Assistance required!" Aldridge called indicating the flags flying on the sloop.

The two pieces of information played at opposite ends of Donland's mind. He was bound by sea law to give assistance but he was almost certain it was a trap, the Narciso being captured or turned over to the Spanish.

Jackson came alongside. Donland's mind still considered his options.

"Sir?" Jackson asked.

"Reduce sail. Just enough for steerage," Donland decided. "We'll keep this distance between us."

He turned to Bill, "How good are your eyes?"

"Good, very good."

"Jackson give him the best glass we have, put a lanyard on it."

"Bill climb to the top of the mainmast, we are going to lie-to. Keep watch and when you see another sail, let me know immediately."

"Aye," Bill answered.

Donland turned his attention to Dewitt in the crosstrees. "Come down Mr. Dewitt."

"You suspect a trap?" Jackson asked.

"Aye," Donland said and repeated what Bill had said about the seemingly wounded sloop.

"She'd make a nice prize."

"Aye, that she would but I fear we'd wind up in the belly of the tiger."

"Sail!" Bill shouted.

Instinctively Donland and Jackson looked up.

"Where away?" Donland called.

Bill pointed with outstretched arm to the southwest.

"As I suspected, that will be either the other sloop or the frigate. Make all sail Mr. Jackson; we shall have to fly to keep that sail from far-reaching us."

"Mr. Dewitt make your course two points to larboard."

"Bill what of the sail?" Donland shouted.

"Frigate!" Bill answered back.

Donland's suspicions were confirmed, but it gave him no satisfaction. His first duty was to secure the dispatches and to prepare them for going overboard. His orders were explicit, "In event of an encounter with superior force take no chances of the dispatches falling into enemy hands." He might well tear the sticks out of *Hornet* avoiding the frigate and her consort but to the admiralty it would be a minor loss compared to the damage of the dispatches he carried in the wrong hands. Messenger he might be but he had served king and country long enough to know that a sloop such as *Hornet* mattered little in the course of a war.

The Spaniards were waiting. Reason held they were not here by accident to capture the unwary. No, someone had passed information that important dispatches were being sent from Boston down to English Harbor and back. The capture of those dispatches would make the allocation of ships and men worthwhile. *Hornet*'s speed and his own cunning would be the difference between the dispatches going to their intended recipients or to their enemies.

Vengador was carrying all the sail she could hold. Her intentions were clear, cut *Hornet* off or drive or towards the sloop. Donland assessed the sloop, she was unfurling more sail.

"Mr. Jackson what of the wind?" he asked.

"It'll hold steady. Yon frigate will have us in long shot distance before we far-reach her. Even if we go about her shot might well carry."

"We press on then," Donland decided.

The distance was closing fast. They would be no match for Vengado in a fight. Every man aboard *Hornet* was doing just as Donland, gauging the distance. At their speed and course it would be a near thing, no more than a half mile to clear the frigate. But, even at that, they would be in range of the frigate's guns long enough for the Dons to fire several long-range shots.

The Narciso had her full set of sails on and was pacing *Hornet.* She was the beater running the quarry to the hunter. There would not be time enough to turn and engage her and escape the frigate. If *Hornet* was to survive, she had to be swift. Donland considered lightening the ship for real but time and distance would make that a useless gesture. He had only minutes not the hour it would take to make enough difference to lighten the ship.

"Your best guess?" Donland asked Jackson.

"Just shy of half-hour."

"Aye," Donland answered.

They could tell that the frigate was altering course slightly to intercept. She would be late but would close the gap enough to tack and bring a broadside to bear within a reasonable distance of her guns. The captain's intent would be to hit enough sail and cordage to slow *Hornet.* He would have no problem closing and capturing with the assistance of Narciso.

"We could try a feint." Jackson suggested.

"He's watching for that. After our last encounter he will be wary of all sail handling. No, he will wait until he is certain of our intentions. Both his broadsides will be loaded and ready for whatever maneuvers we attempt. Our route of escape lies before us. We have better wind; that is our ally, it will have to suffice."

"And his poor gunnery," Jackson added.

Donland saw it before Jackson.

"Slack mizzen topmast!" Jackson shouted.

"One point larboard Mr. Dewitt!" Donland shouted and did not reply to Jackson.

"Wind's fitful from her quarter," Jackson observed.

"Aye, should be enough!" Donland added.

The captain of the frigate lost not a moment as he called for a tack. The loss of wind for only seconds was costing him speed. *Hornet* was going to far-reach.

Jackson was beaming, "he's going to chase us bless his heart."

Hornet was past, the frigate was tacking but her guns would not reach *Hornet.*

"You did it Captain!" Jackson was ecstatic.

Donland did not hear him. His mind was considering another problem. There was another sloop out there somewhere. Narciso was still under full sail and still pacing *Hornet.* But where was the other Spanish sloop?

"Mr. Dewitt, starboard three points!" Donland commanded. He would come back to their original course and gain as much distance as he could from the frigate. Narciso would be faster than the frigate and may even be able to close on *Hornet.* Perhaps drive her toward the other sloop.

Donland looked up and called to Bill who was still as high on the mainmast as a man could climb, "is there another sail?"

The wind carried away Bill's reply but the outstretched arm pointing straight ahead was answer enough.

"Seems we have not escaped our adversaries," Donland said as much to himself as to Jackson.

"Have the gun crews stand ready Mr. Andrews."

"Aye Sir!" Andrews answered and began calling men.

"Mr. Dewitt I will be below. Hold this heading." Donland ordered.

In his cabin he pulled out a chart and began examining it. The sloop ahead of them would be in the middle between Gustavia and Barbuda. Thirty miles to either side and she would be able to match whatever course changes *Hornet* made. Her task would be to slow *Hornet* for the frigate and Narciso to catch up. He estimated *Hornet*'s position, considered his options and put the chart away and started for the hatchway.

"Mr. Dewitt south by southeast if you please," Donland commanded.

"Aye sir," Dewitt answered then added. "Barbuda it is Sir."

Donland studied both the sloop as she tacked on a course to intercept *Hornet* and the tip of Barbuda. Dewitt was doing exactly what he expected which was to keep *Hornet* on a course to run down the western side of Barbuda. He would stay well away from the reefs. The sloop would endeavor to pin *Hornet* to those reefs. By Donland's estimate in less than an hour the Dons would have *Hornet.*

Donland watched the island grow closer and watched as the sloop narrowed the distance. He had second thoughts, perhaps what he intended would not work and *Hornet* would be lost. He reasoned it was too late to change his mind.

"Mr. Dewitt how well do you know the island?" He asked.

Dewitt answered, "Slavers use it. West side is reefs and shoals. Deep water on the east."

"What about the point yonder?" Donland pointed, "how close can we come to it?

Dewitt didn't blink, "If we are to weather it we best be getting about it."

"No channel close in?"

"Aye, was one. I'd not know now, ran tween reefs, maybe forty yards."

"Think the Dons would know of it?"

"Aye, they'd know."

Donland called, "Mr. Jackson reduce sail. Main course only."

"Mr. Andrews bring a gun round to bear as near as you can on that sloop. Fire; full elevation when you are ready."

"Aye Sir!" Andrews replied.

After you fire load both starboard and larboard batteries. Dampen the bags, I want smoke!"

Andrews face registered confusion.

"Dampen the end of the bag away from the touchhole it will cause a great deal of smoke. We shall use it to mask our turn. Be quick about it!"

Hornet began to slow. Donland watched as the sloop also began to reduce sail.

Boom! Andrew's gun sounded.

Donland turned his attention to the sloop. She was slowing anticipating *Hornet* adjusting course to attempt the channel.

Narciso was charging ahead and only cables behind was the Vengado. They had to be certain their quarry was trapped. Flags were racing up and down on Narciso and the Vengado. The sloop was also signaling.

Vengado took the bait and began to tack to run parallel to the channel. Narciso reduced sail to be the stopper in the bottle and the far sloop maintained position thwarting *Hornet*'s ability to change her heading to run south.

Donland moved to stand beside Dewitt. His attention was on the three approaching ships and the nearness of the island. Jackson was shouting orders a few feet away in preparation of wearing ship.

"Mr. Welles my compliments to Mr. Andrews, have him signal me when he is ready."

"Aye Sir!" David replied.

"Mr. Dewitt when I order wear ship bring us around quick as you can. We will fire a broadside at the sloop to our south and immediately fire our other broadside. Set your course south by southwest."

He summoned Jackson with a shout, "When I order wear ship we will come onto a south by southwest heading. Andrews will be firing both batteries."

"But sir the range...!"

Donland cut him short, "Range doesn't matter Mr. Jackson. Hitting the enemy isn't important! On my command!"

Andrews was waving his hat, all was ready.

He turned and gauged the distance to the frigate. He saw their ports begin to open.

"Wear ship!" he shouted loud enough to be heard on the frigate.

The wheel went hard over. "Haul!" Jackson shouted.

Hornet heeled steeply.

"Mr. Andrews fire larboard!" Donland shouted.

There was a slight hesitation and then the guns fired, in a ragged order. All the shots plunged into the sea only a few yards from *Hornet.* The smoke blotted out the sloop.

Hornet still turned, men were cursing and hauling on lines, sails were being run up. Every man aboard worked in confusion.

Donland cupped his hands and shouted, "starboard battery make ready!"

He waited and studied Narciso and Vengado.

"Fire starboard!" Donland shouted.

Again the guns fired in a ragged order. Each shot plunged into the sea after reaching the maximum elevation.

Acrid smoke encircled *Hornet.* She kept turning. Donland hoped the smoke was enough.

Loud booms erupted from nearby. The frigate had fired but there was no shuttering of *Hornet's* hull nor was anything above struck.

Hornet came onto her new course.

"South by southwest!" Dewitt called.

"Cross the sloop's wake Mr. Dewitt!"

"Mr. Jackson make all sail!" Donland called.

Then to Andrews, "Mr. Andrews secure the guns."

A slow roll of thunder erupted. Overhead Donland heard the sounds of sail ripping and lines cracking as they parted. He guessed the sloop had fired as they were approaching her wake. The Dons would get another opportunity if they were quick to tack.

Cordage dropped to the deck. Jackson was shouting, somewhere a man was screaming.

There was a crash and Donland turned in the direction. In the midst of the smoke he saw Narciso tangled with the other sloop and beyond them was the frigate. A cheer rose from the men and many turned to gawk.

"Jump to there!" Jackson shouted, "Dixon move those men, reeve those blocks! Secure that rabble!"

Donland ignored it all; his attention was on the Vengado. She was tacking to come round either to resume the chase or to aid her consorts. In his estimation she would not be able to catch them before reaching English Harbor. Still, now was not the time to reduce sail or to proceed at a leisurely pace. No, even in clear and perfect sailing weather any number of misfortunes might occur.

"Sail!" Bill shouted down.

Donland had forgotten the man was still high up the mainmast.

"Where away?"

Bill pointed directly toward the bowsprit.

Donland took a glass from the rack and began to climb to the cross trees. He knew the ship instantly, *Medusa*! Vengado would not be pursuing them.

After sending and receiving recognition signals, another signal came as a surprise. "Captain repair onboard," Aldridge stated.

"Thank you Mr. Aldridge," Donland said and in the next breath to Jackson. "We will lay-to."

"Samson have the gig lowered."

CHAPTER NINE

Donland came up the side and through the sally port of *Medusa.* He was greeted with a full side party and all the ship's officers. There were smiles on many of the faces of the men he had served with. The marines, serious and proud remained unmoved. After saluting the flag and doffing his hat to the quarterdeck, he presented himself to Captain Okes.

"Mmmph, to my cabin Commander Donland," Okes stated. "Mr. Powell dismiss the side party and come to my cabin."

"Aye Sir," Powell replied.

Donland noticed that there was no joy in Powell, he was certain the man harbored ill feelings from not having been given command of Morgador. Fate some would have called it; other's would say it was God's will. No matter, he was the one to have reaped the rewards and endured the hardships. Powell may have done better but Powell may well have done a good deal worse.

In Okes' cabin, Donland noticed a bottle of wine and three glasses were on the sideboard.

"A toast to your successes," Captain Okes said as he poured wine.

"Thank you Sir," Donland said as he received the glass.

Powell said nothing.

"It occurs to me that I've only been able to toast one of my officers after they received their own command. I must be getting old for I can't remember the man's name. To Commander Donland!" Okes said and lifted his glass.

Powell said nothing and did not drink.

"You are bound for English Harbor?" Okes asked.

"Aye Sir," Donland answered. "Dispatches from Admiral Arbuthnot."

"Still the messenger eh!" Powell at last spoke.

"Aye," Donland replied with a grin. He remembered what Jackson had said and repeated it, "better a messenger boy for the fleet than command of a fourth-rate hulk."

Okes added, "Better first lieutenant of *Medusa* than command of a fourth-rate hulk don't you think Mr. Powell?"

Donland saw the flash of Powell's eyes.

"Aye Sir," Powell did manage to say.

Okes did not miss the anger in Powell either. "In due time Mr. Powell, in due time. Mr. Donland was most fortunate, yours will come in due time, perhaps before sunset tomorrow."

Donland detected something in the way Okes had made the statement. He asked, "Is there to be a battle?"

Okes grinned then answered, "Of sorts, we've received information that there is a dismasted Spaniard drifting off Anguilla. We hope to capture her in the morning."

"Sloop Sir?" Donland asked.

"Aye," Okes answered.

"Beg pardon sir but she's not dismasted," Donland said and then corrected himself. "She was not dismasted at the time you received the information but she may well be by now."

"Explain Sir," Okes insisted.

"We came upon her this morning. We reduced sail to give aid but were suspicious. One of our company recognized her as a captured slaver named Narciso taken by the Spanish. My orders are for a speedy passage and under no circumstances to be delayed. As *Hornet* was about to resume our mission, we observed another a sail approaching and recognized her as the Spanish frigate Vengado. The sloop was bait for a trap. I ordered all sail be put on and we attempted to far reach the frigate and managed to do so. A second sloop was positioned to intercept us before gaining Barbuda. Our company preformed very well, and we were able to evade all three Dons and witnessed the collision of the two sloops. So, as I said, one is probably dismasted or at least considerably damaged."

"When did this happen?" Okes asked.

"Just over an hour ago off Barbuda," Donland answered. "I'm sure *Vengado* gave up the chase after seeing your sail."

"Mmmmph," Okes said and turned away. He pulled a chart. "Here show me."

Donland moved to the chart table and Powell followed. "Donland studied the chart for a moment and then pointed, "there Sir."

"Mmmmph," Okes said again while studying the map. "Two sloops and a frigate!" He mused then asked, "how many guns?"

"Thirty-two, mostly twelve-pounders," Donland answered.

"And the sloops?"

"Ten each, no more than six-pounders."

" Mmmmph," we shall make sail. Commander Donland return to your ship and follow in my lee!"

Donland was stunned. "But Captain Okes...." he protested.

"Sir you have your orders!" Okes countered.
Reluctantly Donland answered, "aye Sir."

Donland was not surprised when the signal came. "Enemy in sight!" What did surprise him was that the *Vengado* was not in sight. The two sloops were as *Hornet* had left them. They had untangled themselves and were making repairs. Their attempt to flee was short-lived as *Medusa* surged to within cannon range and fired her bow chaser. Both commanders of the sloops realized they would not be able to our pace *Medusa* and *Hornet.* They lowered their flags and reduced sail just north of Barbuda.

Hornet took in sail and maintained enough way for steerage. It was in Donland's mind to signal *Medusa* of his intention to return. The sun would be setting within the hour and it would be best to be heading in the direction of Antigua before the light went.

Okes wasted no time sending across boarding parties to claim the prizes. Donland watched from the deck of *Hornet.*

"More's the pity," Jackson stated. "All that prize money going to them buggers."

Donland grinned, "You've had your share first old son."

"Aye!" Jackson replied and admired his new lieutenant's coat. "Aye!" he said again.

"Sail coming round the island!" the lookout called down.

Donland turned and drew the telescope to his eye. "Vengado!" He exclaimed.

Medusa's boats had yet to reach the two sloops. She would be short-handed in a fight and her boats were within range of the sloop's guns.

"Load Mr. Andrews!" Donland shouted. "Load!"

To Jackson he said, "make sail Mr. Jackson!"

Dewitt was standing beside the helmsman. "Put us between the boats and the sloops Mr. Dewitt!"

Overhead sails that had only just been furled were being clewed down. Bill's companions knew their work. They were the finest sail-handlers Donland had ever seen. On this day, they needed to be.

"The Dons are opening ports!" Aldridge exclaimed.

"Hard starboard Mr. Dewitt!" Donland commanded.

To Andrews he shouted, "Mr. Andrews fire any gun that bears!"

Hornet heeled slightly as the wheel went over. It was just enough and Andrews was just in the right place. "Boom!" The six-pounder sounded. Whether by luck or fate the ball hit just aft Narciso's bowsprit. Andrews fired four times more hitting the hull once. One ball tearing through the railing sending splinters into the men nearby.

The men in the boats realized they were in harms way and went over the sides. Donland prayed there were no sharks in the water. What needed to be done had to be done quickly for their sakes.

"Helm hard over larboard! Bring us back on course to that sloop!" he commanded.

There was bumping along *Hornet*'s hull and Donland knew they were among the men who had abandoned the boats. They would be reaching for anything to begin the climb out of the water and onto *Hornet.*

A quick glance at *Medusa* told him that Captain Okes was preparing to meet *Vengado*. Short-handed *Medusa* might be but she had more guns and more men. But *Vengado* had surprise.

Vengado fired a ragged broadside. Most of the balls flew wide of *Medusa* but some hit her but not hard. Whoever was in charge of *Medusa's* guns fired a single gun, then another and on down the line. Donland watched and was certain the shots hit home in *Vengado's* hull.

"She'll not take much of that!" Jackson said in his ear.

Hornet had come on her new heading sailing straight toward *Narciso*. At the same moment, *Narciso* fired her aft three guns and one shot struck *Hornet*'s bow above the waterline.

Dewitt knew his business, without waiting for the command he keeled *Hornet* to starboard to avoid a collision with *Narciso.*

Jackson also knew what was expected of him and shouted orders to take the wind from the sails.

"Grapples!" Donland shouted and precious seconds were lost as men retrieved the grapples. One then two and then several flew across. Four found purchase aboard *Narciso* and were secured.

Hulls banged and Jackson shouted, "boarders to me!" Donland watched as fifteen or more men rushed to the railing and began jumping across. "Mr. Dewitt you have the deck!" Donland shouted as he rushed to join those boarding. He drew his sword and leaped across the gap between the two ships.

A seaman armed with a pike ran at Donland. He hacked the pike and drew the pistol from him belt and clubbed the man. Before he could take on the next man a shout went up. The Spaniard dropped the belaying pin he was holding. It was over; *Narciso's* captain had surrender to Jackson.

Behind him was the roll of cannon fire, slow and deliberate. He turned to see the mizzen of the *Vengado* began to topple. Muskets banged from the tops of *Medusa.* Donland could tell the marines were still out of range but they fired, anyway. Okes would be blistering mad.

The other sloop had not joined the fray. Either her captain was a coward or the damage to his ship's hull was too great to be of any help in the fight.

Again the slow roll of thunder as *Medusa*'s nine-pounders fired. The Spaniard fired two guns.

"Jackson tapped Donland on the shoulder, "Sir," he said and held out a gilded sword.

"Fire! Fire!" Someone shouted.

Donland and Jackson both turned to see flames licking upward on *Vengado's* sails.

"For the love of Christ!" Jackson exclaimed.

There was nothing anyone could do but watch men dive overboard as the flames consumed the ship.

"Secure the prize Mr. Jackson. I shall go across and launch our boats."

"Aye Sir," Jackson replied and thrush the sword out to Donland.

"You won it, keep it," Donland said and climbed onto the railing.

The waning light was devoted to securing the two prizes and pulling men from the water. The second sloop's name was *Gloria*. Her hull was breached in the collision with *Narciso* and she had taken on a considerable amount of water. The *Medusa*'s carpenter and his mates had patched the damaged hull and were pumping. *Narciso*'s battered hull was also being repaired and both ships would be returned to Antigua with *Medusa*. The *Vengado* was still afloat but listed heavily, fires still burned inside.

"She'll be on the bottom before morning," Powell stated.

"Aye," Donland replied sadly.

There was silence in the cabin. They sat there, just the two of them in the two chairs in front of Okes' desk.

Finally, Powell said, "You are senior in rank."

Donland only nodded.

After another long silence Powell asked with formality, "What are you orders Sir?"

Donland knew it was coming and had to be faced. He had already decided but was delaying as long as he could. Powell knew as he did that any decision made concerning command of *Medusa* or the sloops would be only temporary. Admiral Hyde-Parker would make the final decision.

"You will command *Medusa.* Assign one of your lieutenants to *Narciso* and I will send Mr. Andrews over to *Gloria.*" He paused then said, "Ambrose I would if it were mine to do, give you *Medusa* and you know that. If I were certain Hyde-Parker would honor my giving you command of one of the sloops, I would do that. But we both know it is his to decide. In my reports I will speak highly of your sinking the Vengado."

"But I did not sink her! She burned!" Powell interrupted.

"It is my report Ambrose. You were in command after Captain Okes went down and you were the one responsible for the sinking. You commanded and your decisions sank her. Those are the facts and will be in my report. I pray the admiral will reward you with a command of your own as he should. Let there be no more said!"

Weakly Powell said, "aye."

"We shall have Captain Okes burial at first light," Donland said changing the subject.

"Aye." Powell acknowledged.

CHAPTER TEN

Storm clouds were building in the eastern sky as they entered English Harbor. Donland thought it ironic that again he was returning with a small squadron of ships under his command. Tongues would wag all the more but it could not be helped.

Admiral Rowley's flag flew from the admiral's house. Donland assumed he would at last meet the famous commander. It was Lieutenant Lassiter who greeted him at the quay.

"We meet again Sir," Lassiter said with a smile.

"That we do Lieutenant," Donland answered.

Lassiter dropped his smile. "Sir, I must beg your forgiveness for my conduct at our previous encounter."

Donland only nodded.

Admiral Rowley was a gaunt austere man wearing a powered wig and of medium height. Donland knew the man's family linage and was nervous to meet one of England's most distinguished admirals. When he was shown into the admiral's office, Rowley rose from his desk and with a genuine smile said, "welcome Commander Donland." He crossed to Donland and extended his hand. "It's good to meet you. I've been told of your successes. Quite admirable for one so young and young to command."

Donland was speechless.

"Come sit," Rowley commanded as he moved to a chair in front of his desk. "You have dispatches and reports?"

Aye Sir," Donland said as he opened the bag containing his reports and the dispatches.

"The dispatches first if you please," Rowley said.

Donland handed them over and watched as Rowley broke the seals. There were several envelopes and Rowley sorted them.

"Well!" Rowley said in surprise. He held out a small envelope, "This one is for you."

Donland took the envelope, he was astonished. He could not imagine who had sent him a letter in a naval official pouch. He stared at it.

"Well open it, you may as well as I have to give my attention to these," Rowley said.

Donland opened the envelope using his fingernail to lift the wax seal. Inside were two neatly written sheets. It began, "To my Dearest." He read to the end ignoring Rowley and everything. It was signed, Betty Sumerford.

Rowley had not been reading dispatches, he had been watching Donland read and when Donland looked up the admiral was smiling. "Good news from a lady?" he asked.

Dumbfounded Donland managed, "aye Sir."

"Good, good," Rowley said and changed tack, "It is a pity to hear of Captain Okes' death. I met him on two occasions. I understand he died at the beginning of the engagement, is that so?"

"Aye Sir. He brought *Medusa* to action and was killed by the first ball's splinters."

Donland wanted to add that Powell had commanded the ship during the engagement but thought better of it.

"Tell me briefly of the engagement. I shall read your reports later."

Donland did as asked.

Rowley studied him for a moment then asked, "Were you aware that the Spanish ships were operating in that area?"

"Aye Sir, on our passage north we encountered the same three ships, and they had laid an elaborate trap for us."

"You say for us, you mean *Hornet* in particular?"

"I could not say that Sir but I assumed at the time that they were attacking whatever vessel ventured into their trap. I only learned of other encounters when I reached Savannah."

"Were you aware they had captured three of our packet vessels before you encountered them?"

"No Sir, I was not."

"Admiral Welles did well to assign you to the task. Our communications were greatly hampered by that frigate and her consorts. I shall read your reports with great interest. But they will have to wait until I have digested the news from Vice Admiral Arbuthnot and the other commanders. Good day to you commander and well done."

Donland started to rise and resettled himself in the chair. "Sir, before I go I need to make mention of Mr. Powell's command of *Medusa* during the engagement. He acquitted himself with honor after the death of Captain Okes. He sank Vengado, the frigate."

Rowley looked peeved, "Thank you Commander, you can go now."

Donland rose and strode to the door.

"Commander, provision your ship. I'll have dispatches for Admiral Hyde Parker and you'll sail on the tide tomorrow morning."

"Aye Sir," Donland answered. He was still the fleet's messenger boy. He thought to himself, better than commanding a fourth-rate hulk.

The End

Book 2 - Donland's Ransom is available

Made in the USA
Las Vegas, NV
06 December 2024